Not So Happily Ever After

Theastarr Valerie

Empress Royále
Publishing

Not So Happily Ever After
Copyright © 2020 Theastarr Valerie

Editors: Theastarr Valerie, Akilah Valerie – Empress Royále Publishing

Email: empressroyalepublishing@gmail.com

Cover Design: Empress Royále Publishing

Cover Photo: "Gift Tags" from StockSnap (Pixabay.com)

Empress Royále Publishing

"Everything tells a story; let us help you tell your story to the world."

Email: empressroyalepublishing@gmail.com

To My Sisters

The doctors said that you wouldn't live beyond 13 years old, but here you are...

Happy 25th Birthday Akilah aka Da Ladii.

Happy 30th Birthday Aleah aka Princess.

I thank God for your lives.

I pray that you become all that God has created you to be. May God bless you with many more years.

Love,

~Your big sis, Theastarr aka Empress T

Chapter

1

*T*ahira Mikos sluggishly opens the car door and saunters up the steps to her matrimonial home. She knew that her husband would be waiting with a barrage of questions. Wiping the tears from her eyes, she turns the key in the lock.

"What did the doctor say?" Tavario asks, the moment she enters the foyer.

"I don't want to talk about it," she replies, trying to ignore his stare.

"I'm your husband, you can tell me anything."

"I'm sorry that I can't give you your heart's desire," Tahira sobs.

Tavario smiles at his wife. "You are my heart's desire."

"Children, Tavario. I'm talking about children."

Tavario takes his wife's hands and whispers, "In God's time we'll have children. You're the mother of nations, *Dolcezza*."

"Don't call me that. This is humiliating. We've been trying for months."

"What did the doctor say?" Tavario repeats.

"I'm messed up on the inside."

"Those are strong words." Tavario looks into her eyes. "I love you Empress and we'll overcome any obstacle. Look at our journey to the altar. God did that. HE didn't change. What did the doctor say?"

Tahira pulls away from her husband's embrace. "Stop badgering me. I can't do this with you. Divorce me and marry someone who isn't barren."

"We've spoken about your negative words during our devotions, Tahira."

"It's easy for you to say. Nothing's wrong with you. But, **I am damaged goods**."

"I know this isn't easy, but please speak positive into the atmosphere," Tavario tries to comfort her. *"Life and death is in the power of the tongue.* I'm going to continue declaring that you are a mother until it happens. Don't be discouraged."

"Just stop," she snaps.

Tavario washes the glass he picked up from the table. He proceeds to go upstairs to their bedroom. "When you're ready to speak you know where to find me."

As his foot touches the first stair, Tahira blurts out, "I have Polycystic Ovary Syndrome."

The next morning Tahira wakes up with a migraine from a night's worth of tears. She touches her husband's side of the bed. When she doesn't feel him, she begins to panic, calling out his name.

Tavario enters the room with a tray of food. "I'm here *Dolcezza.* I made you breakfast. You went to sleep in agony and I wanted you to have a better morning. I'll wait while you complete your cleansing routine."

Tahira stares at the plate and wrinkles her nose. "I'm not hungry. I don't want to eat anything that would flare up my cysts."

"Stop that," Tavario utters.

"What did I say?"

"Stop claiming diseases. Jesus Christ didn't die on the cross for you to claim infirmities. I rebuke PCOS in the name of Jesus."

Tahira crumples the bedsheet, seething in anger. "Facts are facts Tavario."

"I choose to believe God's report and HIS word says *by HIS stripes you are healed.*"

Sitting up in the bed, Tahira glares at her husband and with low sobs says, "Then explain to me why I can't get pregnant."

"It's not the time, that's all."

"Are you saying you'll stay with me even if I never get pregnant?"

"I'm honoring my vows. I promise I'm not leaving you. No matter what happens. I love you."

"That's what you say now. Give it time and we'll see. I'm going for a jog. I need to clear my head. No food for me."

Chapter

2

4 *Not So Happily Ever After*

*T*ahira observes herself in the mirror, while gently rubbing her stomach. The daily battle of infertility plagued her mind. Ever since their wedding a little over a year ago, they tried to conceive.

Both her parents and in-laws constantly asked about their grandchild. No one understood the pressure of being barren at 29. Of course she didn't share her feelings with her husband. Guilt and shame overwhelmed her.

PCOS was not an expected diagnosis. Prior to their nuptials, they went to the doctor for a thorough medical checkup. The results came back in their favor. Nothing should have stopped them from conceiving.

Their anniversary came and went like any other day. They opted to celebrate in April instead of January. Originally, they'd planned to go on an all-inclusive vacation, but then Tahira got sick and spent a week in the hospital. She avoided going to the doctor for a few days until Tavario insisted.

Weekly date nights were an important part of their marriage. After dodging the conversation, Tahira finally agreed to a date night to make up for their failed vacation.

When they got in the car, she peers out the window in silence.

Tavario touches her hand. "*Dolcezza*, why are you silent?"

"I don't want to go anywhere," Tahira snaps.

"Why are you pushing me away?"

"You speak of loving me with your words, but I can see it in your eyes how much I disgust you."

"I love you. But, you've put up a resistance against me, ever since you returned from the doctor."

"Everywhere we go I see the look on your face around children. Like you wish you were a father."

"We have time. I'm not sure why you're worried," he responds, keeping his eyes on the road.

"The doctor said I can't have any children because of my condition."

"We're going to get a second opinion. I pray that you stop speaking negative. You don't have PCOS. Don't declare that."

"You're not a medical professional."

Tavario parks the car in front of the restaurant, turns to his wife and responds, "And medical professionals aren't God. Misdiagnosis happens all the time."

Tahira and her husband ate in silence. When they were both finished, Tavario excuses himself from the table to answer a phone call.

Tahira uses her fork to scrape the leftover food on her plate from side to side.

"Would you like to see the dessert menu?"

Tahira looks at the waitress. "Do you have anything that can help a woman become pregnant?"

"Excuse me?"

"Are you interested in being a surrogate mother?"

With a shocked expression, the waitress responds, "Are you alright ma'am? If you're drunk I can call a taxi to take you home."

"I'm not drunk, just barren."

"I don't know who you are, but you shouldn't say things like that. Words are powerful and you should be careful of what you say. I'll give you a few minutes to decide," the waitress replies.

When Tavario returns to the table, Tahira glares at him. "Who was that on the phone?"

"Someone from an agency asking me to conduct a seminar," he answers flatly.

"Since when are you so secretive with me? Does this person have a name?"

"L-something, I can't remember. I have to call back for further details—"

Just then a boy taps his shoulder. "Excuse me sir. Are you Tavario Mikos?"

A woman clutches the boy and stares at Tavario apologetically, "I'm sorry for interrupting. My son is a huge fan of your movies."

Tavario smiles at the lady. "It's not a problem miss." He turns to the boy. "What's your name?"

"Justice," the boy announces proudly. "*Triple Retaliation* and *War of Doors* are my favorite movies."

"What a powerful name," Tavario commends. "Why thank you, I'm glad you like them."

"Come on Justice; let's leave Mr. Mikos to finish his dinner," his mother nods.

Yanking his hand away from his mother, Justice continues, "Can you sign this menu for me? I want to show my friends at school."

Tavario signs the menu.

"Again sorry for the interruption," Justice' mother reiterates as they leave the table.

"Enjoy the rest of your evening," Tavario waves.

Tahira stares at her husband, annoyed.

So everyone's going to act like I wasn't sitting here the entire time? He didn't even introduce me? What is happening?

Arguing with Tahira was not something that Tavario took pleasure in. He always looked to God for guidance. The drive back home was awkward and his wife continued giving him the cold shoulder.

Tavario goes into his prayer closet to pray for his wife and their marriage. As he knelt down, he blinked a few times. Sleep would not prevent his prayer.

For some reason he couldn't shake the feeling that something was about to turn his world upside down. He shook the feeling off and prayed...

> *"Dear God,*
>
> *I come to You in the name of Jesus. I thank You for who You are. Thank You for the wife that You've blessed me*
> *with. Lord Jesus, I pray that you give me the wisdom to deal with whatever Tahira is going through. I ask that You*
> *show me the right way to speak to her. Let her know how much I love her, but most importantly how much You love her. I come against this negative feeling that I have even now. Help me to maintain my calm. Help me to honor my marriage vows. Guide me. In Jesus' name I pray. Amen."*

It was 1AM and Tahira hadn't entered the bedroom she shared with her husband. They'd returned from dinner around 10:30 and she decided to stay in the car and cry. Tavario tried to console her, to no avail. She deliberately ignored him. How could a man love her so much? Yes, she'd read in the Bible that husbands were to love their wives as Christ loves the church, but she couldn't fathom why her husband loved her.

She knew that she needed to speak to Jesus, but didn't have the strength to enter any prayer chamber. Every night since her diagnosis (just like every night since they started courting) Tavario would pray on her behalf. Not only was he a man of integrity, but also a man of prayer.

After he exited the car, Tahira took out her phone and watched a movie, not knowing when she fell asleep. At 11:45PM she woke up and found herself on the living room couch under a blanket. She'd heard Tavario praying upstairs. He'd obviously come back to the car and carried her inside.

My husband is good to me. He doesn't deserve the life he's living with me as a barren wife.

Chapter

3

11 *Not So Happily Ever After*

*T*he following afternoon, Tahira calls her mother.

"Hi sweetie, what's the matter?" Tahiti asks.

"I think my marriage is over," Tahira exclaims.

"What happened?"

"I went to the doctor and he told me that I have PCOS."

"Are you claiming it?" her mother queries.

Agitated, Tahira replies, "I'm not claiming anything, but it's what the doctor said."

"Do you feel any pain? Do you have a regular period?"

"No and yes, I had my period last month."

Tahiti sighs over the phone. "I believe that you should get a second opinion. Don't declare an end to your life because of it. It could be a misdiagnosis."

"Why would the doctor lie?"

"It may not be a lie, but human error; tiredness, misreading of results. He could've picked up someone else's chart by mistake. There are many possibilities. All I'm saying is get a second opinion and don't accept **any** disease or illness. You're a child of God," Tahiti counters.

"What explanation is there for me being unable to conceive?" Tahira asks. "I can see it all over my husband's face. He wants to have children. We went out for dinner last night and a boy came up to him.

Tavario's entire demeanor changed, like a proud father. It was weird. And it wasn't the only time."

"You both want to have children. That's one of the reasons you got married. You'll make wonderful parents someday."

"Why are you pressuring us then?"

"No one's pressuring you. You know I've wanted grandbabies forever and I'm sure Avela has as well."

"Tavario's mother already has grandchildren."

"Not from her firstborn son."

"This is too much," Tahira whines. "I feel like I'm being punished."

"Look sweetie," her mother counters, "just because things aren't going according to your timeline doesn't mean that you won't have a baby. You need to trust God."

"Easy for you to say, you had me nine months after you married daddy."

"That was our journey. Yours is different. When the time is right you will have children."

Tahira rolls her eyes. No one truly understood how she felt and she was tired of trying to explain herself. "I'm going now, the oven timer rang. Later mom, I love you."

"Later sweetie, I love you."

Chapter

4

*T*wo days later, when Tavario walks into the house, he greets his wife with a kiss. Instead of returning his passion, she pushes him away and increases the volume on the TV.

Tavario takes the remote and mutes the TV. "What's the matter Tahira?"

She elevates off the couch. "Your dinner's in the oven. I'm going to bed."

"Please stay *Dolcezza*."

"Don't *Dolcezza* me," she snaps. "I'm furious with you."

"I know. This is the first time you've spoken to me in two days."

"Tavario, look me in my face and answer honestly. Are you having an affair?"

Her husband's eyes open wide, shocked at the accusation. "Where is this coming from?"

"You've been getting a lot more phone calls lately. Plus you haven't been upfront with me about this *L-something* person. And if that isn't bad enough, a few nights ago I had a dream about another woman giving you a paternity test stating that **YOU ARE THE FATHER**. Who is this woman?"

"Are you accusing me of cheating because of a dream?"

"My dreams have been spot on in the past. I trust them."

15 *Not So Happily Ever After*

"Tahira, sometimes our feelings cloud our mind and what we dream is a result of our waking conflict."

"You're not a dream analyst," she scoffs.

"I don't want to argue with you."

"Then tell me the name of the woman you've been seeing and receiving calls from."

"What is there to hide?" he asks. "We both have one another's passwords for all our accounts. You can check whatever you want."

"Always Mr. Confident," Tahira replies, standing akimbo. "The guilty ones are always the most confident."

"Can I just eat and relax? I don't want to argue."

"You **never** want to do anything with me anymore. Some husband you are."

"You push me away every time I try," Tavario exhales.

"Do you even know my *love language*?"

"What is the use of speaking someone's love language if that person has blocked themselves off?"

"You got some NERVE mister. Some nerve. Go eat your dinner, I don't care."

"I'll speak to you when you're calm. I'm not entertaining your negativity," Tavario retorts.

Immediately after the argument with Tavario, Tahira calls Kaiora Canzoniere, her best friend since adolescence. Kaiora was one of the few people she knew would be honest with her, along with her parents; even though she didn't readily admit it.

She was married to a missionary, Pastor Amerigio and they had two children: Nizelli and Nayoro-Kaimeri.

"Kaiora, you've been married longer than I have, how do you deal with a man who ignores you?"

"Let's talk about the text you sent before you called me."

"Why? That was just an update, I want to vent."

"Girl you know I'll tell you the truth. Don't ignore this. You sent that text for a reason."

Tahira sucks her teeth. "Fine, go ahead. You won't be Kaiora if you don't speak your mind."

"Tavario loves you and would never cheat on you. I agree with everyone, get a second opinion. You're not in any pain nor are you showing the dominant symptoms of PCOS, so get another opinion. I know of women whose doctors claimed they would never be able to conceive and they went on to have as much as a dozen children."

"Do you know those women personally?" Tahira stresses.

"Yes, I met one while on a mission trip in Spain. She's about 70 years old now," Kaiora informs.

"That's a one in a million chance."

"Girl, cut that out. I know you love to drag on your pity parties, but it isn't doing you any good. You'll stress yourself out and lash out at Tavario. It's not necessary."

"How is your family?" Tahira retorts, changing the subject.

"Everyone's great. Nizelli will be starting 1A Elementary in the fall when we move to Lucca."

"I still can't believe you're moving to Italy."

"It's our mission field. An opportunity has opened for Amerigio to Pastor a Church there and we've prayerfully accepted."

"My best friend's moving halfway across the world," Tahira sighs.

"You know you can come visit me. We'll be back and forth between there and Starr Islands until I settle things here. No big deal. It's what we've been doing for almost a decade."

"I know Kaiora. I'll miss you. I have to come visit you in Kalanailani before you move."

"Forget all that. We're coming to *Saheluna* to see you and Tavario."

"He may not be around when you come. You'll have to settle for plain ol' me."

"Let's pray. I know you're going through a tough trial, but God is able to see you through..."

Chapter

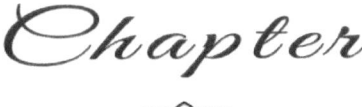

5

19 *Not So Happily Ever After*

*O*ne week passed and their marital spat hadn't subsided. Tavario had had enough. Their days and nights were filled with cold shoulders.

Today in particular, instead of a warm breakfast, Tahira left a bowl of *Medallion Cereal* and a cup of *Lavender Milk* on the kitchen island, along with a note.

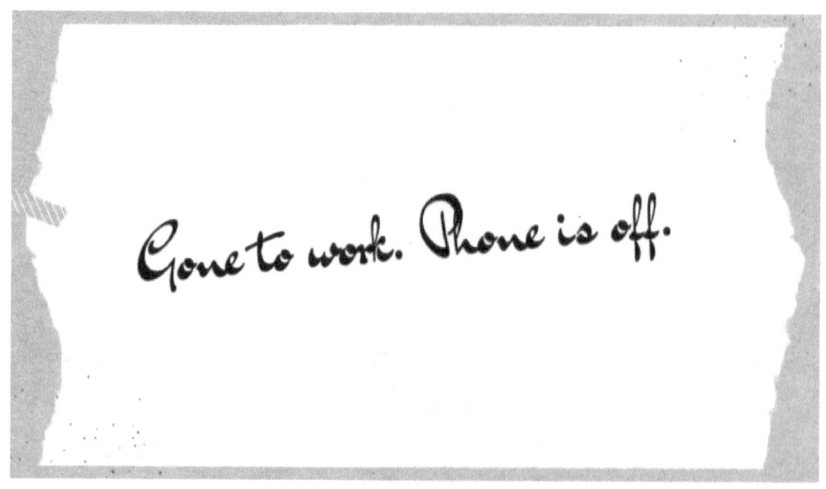

Gone to work. Phone is off.

Dry. Simple. With no love. Even though he knew that his wife took the diagnosis hard, he didn't want to give up on their marriage.

He continued to do his job as Missions Director while she was CEO of *Tahinaiza Travel Agency*. Her company was a combination of her first, middle, and maiden names: **Tah**ira **In**ielle **Ai**yoki **Za**gori.

Tavario was proud of his wife and they both supported one another. Her agency assisted missionary teams around the globe with their travel plans. They were a tag team until two weeks ago.

His best friends, Amerigio Canzoniere and Xylon Yarbrough gave him advice to help patch things up, but Tahira wouldn't budge. So they continued their weekly prayer calls for one another as they navigated the world of marriage, family, ministry, and career.

Amerigio left for Lucca, Italy to Pastor *Chiesa del Regno* and Xylon was officially an Agent in the NIU. Having a likeminded brotherly bond was what he needed.

The day Xylon, Olympia, and Siren got baptized was a cause for celebration at the Mikos' household. Their conversion took place at a church in Greece, a few months after Tavario and Tahira got married.

Xylon, Olympia, and Siren, were working undercover with Church officials to capture a criminal who kidnapped local children. This meant spending a lot of time hearing God's word. At the end of the mission they all gave their hearts to Christ.

After his walk down memory lane, Tavario decides to go visit his wife at work to make amends. No couple should spend that much time not truly communicating with one another.

At the agency, Tavario is greeted by the receptionist. "Mr. Mikos, your wife is on a call at the moment. Is she expecting you?"

"Not to worry, I'll quietly let myself in."

"Suit yourself; you know where her office is," the receptionist says, resuming her typing.

From the hallway, Tavario observes his wife smiling as she speaks on the phone. He loved viewing her in her element.

When he enters the room, he is greeted by an icy stare. Tahira mutes the phone and rolls her eyes. "What are you doing here?"

"Finish your call, I'll wait," Tavario replies, taking a seat.

"I'm going to call you back. Someone just showed up." Tahira angrily hangs up the phone.

"*Someone?*" Tavario scoffs. "I'm your husband."

"I don't have time for this. Why are you here?"

"Let's go out to lunch. We haven't been on a date in a while."

"I'm busy," Tahira states.

"Why have I become the enemy in your eyes?"

Tahira balls up a fist. "Tavario, I'm AT WORK if you don't mind. I don't want to speak to you. Nor do I want to have lunch with you. You're annoying me."

"I know you're under an immense amount of duress. Please talk to me. Share with me. You know that I love you."

"You sound pathetic. Can I go back to my call now? I have a business to run." She picks up the phone and turns her back.

"So you're really not going to say anything to me?"

Tahira scoffs as she continues her phone call. "I'm so sorry about that. What dates were you interested in

traveling again? Uh huh, okay, okay. Let's make it happen then..."

Chapter

6

24 *Not So Happily Ever After*

*I*t was 5PM and his wife hadn't returned from work. Tavario was just about to head to his home office when the doorbell rang.

Tavario opens the door to a blast from the past. The visitor was unwelcomed.

"How'd you get this address?" he snaps.

"Good evening to you too," the woman flirts. "I mean your address is hardly private. You're a big shot Missions Director in *Saheluna*. Your secretary gave me your information. I told her it's important."

"Nova, I don't think it's a wise idea for you to come in. It's been over five years since I've seen you. What do you want?"

"You really **have** left the acting circuit behind. At least be courteous and invite me to sit down. Lovely porch you have. Real homey," Nova laughs seductively. "Shall we sit?"

"Sit over there," Tavario points. "Not too close."

"I see I still get under your skin. Just like old times," Nova winks.

"Don't disrespect my wife or marriage. What we had is ancient history."

"May not be as ancient as you think."

"What are you talking about?"

Nova hands Tavario a photo of a boy. "Do you know him?"

Tavario begins to feel even more uncomfortable. "No."

"Look closely."

"What are you getting at?"

"His name is Haselt."

"And—"

"He's your son..."

Pulling into the driveway, Tahira stares at the woman on her porch.

What is SHE doing here?

Tahira hastily walks up the stairs and begins yelling. "ARE YOU KIDDING ME, TAVARIO? OUT OF ALL THE WOMEN ON THIS PLANET— NOVA? YOU CHEAT ON ME WITH YOUR EX?"

"Good night **commoner**. I see you've won the ring," Nova teases.

"I'm not speaking to you," Tahira growls. "Tavario, why are you just standing there with your mouth open? Say something."

"Oh, I can tell you why—"

Tahira exhales. "I said I'm not speaking to you, *NO-VA*."

Nova grins and throws her head back. "You'll be doing a lot more speaking to me in years to come."

Tahira looks to her husband for answers. "What is she talking about?"

He tries to speak but no words come out.

"TAVARIO, WHAT IS SHE TALKING ABOUT?" Tahira barks.

Nova hands Tahira the photo of the boy and walks to her car. "That's Haselt Duesing, Tavario's 7 year old son. Tavario, I'll be back so that we can discuss custody rights and all the child support checks you owe me." Nova slams the car door and drives off.

Inside the living room Tahira paces back and forth in tears trying to formulate words. Then she stands akimbo. "YOU HAVE A SON?"

"I don't know what is happening. But, it's impossible. You have to believe me."

"No. No. It's not impossible. You were with Nova years before you met me. I remember her coming around that time we were at *Holbrook Resort and Spa*. That was perfect timing to have a little rendezvous. How long were you going to hide that you're a father from me? Do your parents know?"

"She's lying. The age of her son doesn't add up to when last we... you know."

"I don't expect you'd remember that far back."

"Why would she wait all these years to reveal that I'm her child's father? I know Nova, she would've told me the moment she found out she was pregnant."

27 *Not So Happily Ever After*

"I don't CARE what reasoning she has. You fathered a child with another woman and now you're trying to play mathematician?"

Tavario begins to plead. "Don't you see what's happening?"

"Yes, you got your wish. You're a **father** now. Go be with Nova and leave me alone."

"The enemy has used our quarrel as an opportunity to break up our marriage permanently."

Tahira laughs sarcastically. "How original: your ex of all people. I don't want to hear your fake theory. I'm calling a divorce lawyer, first thing tomorrow morning. You are no longer my husband."

"*Dolcezza*, you have to believe me. She's lying."

"Don't TOUCH ME!" she snaps.

Chapter

7

29 *Not So Happily Ever After*

*T*he argument between Tahira and Tavario continued for hours even while she packed her suitcase. At 9:30PM she hoisted her suitcase down the stairs.

"*Dolcezza,* please don't do this," Tavario begs.

"I've been humiliated enough in my early twenties. I'm not entering my thirties in disgrace. You'll just become a part of my exes."

"God has been good to you in spite of all you've been through, yet you keep bringing up past pain."

"Save your sermon. I don't want to hear it." She begins to roll her suitcase towards the door, stopping briefly to wipe her tears. "Goodbye Tavario."

Five minutes to midnight, after checking into a hotel on the outskirts of the city, Tahira walks to the window in her rental apartment and sighs. Here she was at 29 years old, on the verge of a divorce. Who'd have ever thought that their road of love would end so soon?

She decided to do a short-term rental agreement for two months. Then she would figure out her life. Of course they'd vowed to stay together in *good times and bad,* but this situation was too much.

I don't know what to do. My life is ruined. Hopefully my lawyer can speed up these divorce proceedings. I don't want anything from Tavario, except my dignity. I hope the tabloids doesn't get a hold of this and make a field day out of it. That's what I get for marrying someone who was in the limelight. A woman like Nova is sure to bring him back into it.

Chapter

8

Jozelle Oasis, Fortazonio

July

*T*he day after her rental agreement was up, Tahira calls her parents. She made arrangements to stay with them in Fortazonio, until she found a new place to live.

When Tahiti opens the door, she hugs her daughter and ushers her in the house. "I'm happy that you're spending time with us, but not under these circumstances. When last did you speak with your husband?"

"Hi mom, am I not welcomed here?"

"You're always welcome sweetie. How long are you staying?"

"I don't know. I can do my work from here."

"What about Tavario?"

Tahira shrugs. "He's called numerous times. I haven't responded. I changed my number."

"I've made *Peanut Coconut Parfait*, do you want a glass until dinner's finished?" Tahiti asks, noting the hesitance on her daughter's face.

"I'm good thanks. Where's dad?"

"Your father went to the hardware store to buy some materials. He wants to make a gazebo for us in the backyard."

"Good ol' dad, always the romantic."

"I love my Ramiro."

"Mushy."

Tahiti scoops out some parfait for herself, and then turns to Tahira. "How do you feel? Did that woman contact Tavario again, concerning his possible son?"

"Mom, I just said I haven't spoken to him and honestly I don't care."

"You need to. Tavario is your husband and you made vows. I know you didn't wait twenty years to marry your *dream guy* only to give up after one year and an issue."

"This isn't just some petty issue, it's a **child**."

"Do you have proof that the boy is his child? Even if he is, the child was created **before** you and Tavario even started courting. You can't blame him for his past."

Tahira glares at her mother. "You're taking his side?"

"I've been with the same man for over thirty years. I know a thing or two and then some about other women, lies, schemes, and plotting," Tahiti reveals.

"Daddy cheated on you?"

"No he didn't. But, women have tried to come between us."

"How did you deal with it?"

"Prayer."

"I know God is able to fix any situation, but my marriage is over. I can't give my husband a child so someone else came and presented one to him."

"Wake up baby girl. You're in a spiritual battle. Do not allow the enemy to mess up what God has joined together."

"I brought this on myself," Tahira sighs. "I told Tavario to divorce me and find a woman who can give him a child. And BOOM here comes his ex, Nova Duesing; a supermodel."

"It doesn't matter who she is. You're Mrs. Tavario Mikos, not her. You'd better repent for what you've said."

"What good is it? It's already been spoken."

"God forgives us when we're truly repentant. HE also has mercy upon us for our ignorance."

"Even with all that, I can't be with a man who fathered another woman's child."

"One he may have had before you met?"

"Doesn't matter. There are certain things I can deal with. This isn't one of them."

"You're going to work things out with your husband," Tahiti says. "As long as you're living under this roof the **D** word is not to be uttered. We promote **marriage**. And you will be present at every Church service; including Women's All Night Prayer Meeting—"

"Okay mom, whatever you say. Just please drop the marriage talk."

"You're not off the hook that easily."

"I'm going to my room," Tahira scoffs.

Chapter

9

37 *Not So Happily Ever After*

"*I* see you've been avoiding me and my calls," Nova snaps, two days later. She'd called Tavario to discuss child support.

"I'm a married man. For months I've asked for a DNA test to be done and you've refused," Tavario retorts, aggravated.

"I don't need a test to prove that Haselt is your son. I know who my child's father is. It's you."

"That phrase has been said many times to men. When it turned out the child wasn't even theirs. What makes this any different?"

"Not my problem," Nova scoffs. "I refuse to be part of the **Baby Mama** statistic. You're going to divorce Tahira and marry me."

"Are you hearing yourself? I'm not divorcing my wife."

"Yet, she's nowhere to be found. Do you even know where she is?"

"My marriage isn't any of your business."

"I need to know what type of roof Haselt would be living under when he's with his father. However, if we're married I wouldn't have any reservations."

"Then let's do the DNA test," Tavario responds.

"You're insulting me. Let's change the subject. I've realized that flying back and forth every weekend for the past month is too expensive. Can we stay with you?"

Tavario pauses and a question comes to mind. "Where is Haselt at this moment?"

"With a nanny."

"You wouldn't be wasting all this money if you go back home."

"I'd gladly do that Tavario, if you'd give me the child support money that you owe. Then I'd have enough to take care of him."

"I wouldn't have a problem taking care of Haselt, if he's my son. Let's do the DNA test."

"I said NO already. Why don't we set up a day for us to hang out so you can get to know one another as **father** and **son**?"

No longer able to tolerate Nova's antics, Tavario hangs up the phone.

"Kaiora, do you know where Tahira is?" Tavario asks after he ended his call with Nova.

"I do, but I promised her I wouldn't say anything."

"I miss my wife. Where is she? Please tell me."

"She's my best friend. I want to honor her wishes."

"You were the Maid of Honor at our wedding. Therefore, you heard our vows and stood as witness in agreement. She's my wife. I shouldn't have to beg you to divulge this information."

"You're putting me in a bad position," Kaiora laments.

"What if something happens to her? You know where she is."

"She said that you hurt her. I can't allow you to hurt her."

Tavario sighs. "Do you honestly believe I'd hurt my Empress?"

"Hey, people are capable of anything."

"I love my wife and you know that. Please tell me where she is."

Hearing the obvious distress in his voice, Kaiora exhales, "She's in Fortazonio, by her parents."

"Thank you."

Kaiora hangs up the phone and immediately calls her best friend.

"He called again. I've avoided it long enough, but Amerigio insisted that I answer his call. They've been praying for you."

"For what?" Tahira snaps.

"You know Amerigio, Tavario, and Xylon have their brotherly prayer meeting once a week. Well Tahira, you've been a priority on their prayer list."

"I wish he'd stop making a big deal about this."

"You expect Mr. Tavario E. Mikos **not** to make a BIG DEAL about his *Dolcezza?* His Empress? Who do you think you married?"

"This is not funny."

"I'm being serious. The man loved you even before he knew it."

"People change."

"Don't give me that nonsense. You **know** without a doubt that he loves you."

"It doesn't make that woman and her baby go away."

"You're saying you're willing to give up twenty plus years
of loving a man and one year of marriage because of some woman and her accusations about her son's paternal heritage?" Kaiora pauses, then continues with emphasis, "There's NO PROOF that baby is his. NONE."

"You sound like my mother."

"We've always been rational. Think about how you're sounding right now."

"Whatever. Anyways, the headache has returned and the pain in my stomach has worsened."

"When was your last period?"

"Months ago."

"You're pregnant."

"The doctor said my symptoms are PCOS related. Not having a regular period is part of it."

"Then you need to get a second opinion."

"That **was** from a second opinion. I went to an OBGYN here in Fortazonio."

"Okay then. I'm sorry that you're in pain. I will continue to pray for you."

"Thanks Kaiora. I need all the prayers I can get."

"Before I go, can I add something?"

"Sure."

"If Tavario comes to visit **please** don't shun him. A lot of women would give their last to have a husband with even ten percent of the caliber yours has. Don't take him for granted."

"Not making any promises; since they're clearly worthless in our friendship," Tahira counters, referring to Kaiora revealing her whereabouts.

"I did what was needed under the circumstances. Tavario loves you."

Ignoring Kaiora's warning, Tahira ends the conversation with, "Give my nephew and niece a hug for me. Tell Amerigio I said hi."

Chapter

10

43 *Not So Happily Ever After*

*T*he following afternoon, Tahira opens the door to the backyard, shielding her face from the beaming midday sun.

Ramiro was busily putting together the gazebo. He wipes sweat off his brows.

"Good afternoon daddy, I brought you a cold glass of *Blitz*. It's a scorcher out here."

"Tell me about it. Rainy season, yeah right," Ramiro jokes.

She picks up a hammer. "Can I help?"

"What do you know about carpentry, young girl?" he states, mimicking a country accent.

"Hardy har har. You taught me well."

Ramiro sips his drink and places the glass on a nearby work table. "Sit, let's talk. I know you didn't come out here to do construction work. What's on your mind?"

"Tavario."

"I try not to get in your business. I always believe married couples should solve their own issues with God's help. But, as your father I must say this is **ridiculous**."

"What is?"

"You being here, leaving your husband alone in another country. You RUNNING away like you did when you were younger. I love you sweetie, but I don't condone this folly one bit. You need to go back to your husband."

"It's not that easy."

"Marriage is not easy. That's why it's grown folks business. You've been through too much with Tavario to let anyone come between you. He's like a son to me and I know he loves you."

"No one doubts his love. But, it doesn't excuse the embarrassing mess we're in. It doesn't remove the elephant in the room... my *infertility*."

"As a man of prayer I'm not worried. I'll keep praying for you like I've been doing since the day your mother told me she was pregnant."

"Why does it seem like you're taking his side?" Tahira complains.

"There are no sides in marriage, my child. Go work things out with your husband. All these months and you've left him to live alone? You don't think there are women vying for his attention, besides Nova?" her father scolds.

"Oh well, he can do whatever he wants. Whether I'm there or not he will."

"That's the wrong mindset. You'd better deal with it before it's too late. I don't mind you staying with us, but you need to be with your husband. You're almost 30 not 18. Go fix it."

"I'm not ready."

Ramiro takes her hands. "Let's pray because Lord **knows** what I've had to put up with you as my daughter. It's Tavario's turn. You need to go back to your husband."

Is my father trying to be funny at a time like this?

Chapter

11

47 *Not So Happily Ever After*

*L*ater that night, the phone buzzes on Tavario's desk. He picks up after three rings.

"Have you heard from her yet?" Amerigio asks.

Amerigio was one of Tavario's best friends, whom he trusted wholeheartedly.

"No," Tavario mumbles into the receiver.

"You've truly endured a lot my brother."

"She changed her phone number."

Amerigio clears his throat. "What about going to see her?"

"I didn't know where she was."

"But you do now. Go see her."

"She won't have me."

"You're her husband," Amerigio asserts.

"Not according to her."

"This is not the Tavario I know."

"Have you ever had an argument with Kaiora?" Tavario looks out the window while waiting for his friend's response.

"Are you kidding me? My wife's feisty."

Tavario chuckles, "True."

"No marriage is without issues; don't let anyone tell you otherwise."

"Care to share? It'll really help hearing from an expert like you."

"I'm no expert, believe me. It is only the grace of God that has kept us. Do you know Kaiora almost left me?"

"What?" Tavario exclaims. "When?"

"After we returned from our honeymoon and reality set in. She told me she wasn't qualified to be a Pastor's wife. And she compared herself to many of the wives in the church."

"How did you resolve the issue?"

"It came at a high price. I told her to be herself. That only God could define her and that HE loved her and would use her for HIS Kingdom. She just had to trust HIM. I also did some introspection to see what I could do to help her transition. I decided to cut down on my work hours and we went on fewer mission trips until she felt comfortable enough to continue."

Tavario sighs. "You make it sound easy."

"It's not. My wife is the most important person to me and I aim to show her that daily."

"I've tried with Tahira. What else can I do?"

"Show her that you're willing to fight for your marriage. Show her that you love her. Women pay attention to **everything**. Even though she may be upset with you at this point, you don't want it to look like you didn't try everything."

"Amerigio, I've tried all I can. She isn't budging."

"You know your wife more than I do. Prayerfully go and ask her to come home with you. Continue pursuing her. Too many men stop pursuing their wives after they get married. Go and pursue your wife."

"I will. Thanks for the help, Amer."

"Anytime bro. Book that ticket tonight."

Chapter

12

51 *Not So Happily Ever After*

*T*he phone call with Amerigio gave Tavario the extra jolt of confidence he needed to call his wife. After pacing the foyer for ten minutes, he punched in the numbers for the Zagori house. It felt strange calling his in-laws to speak with Tahira, but it was the beginning of his last resort efforts.

"How are you my son?" Ramiro answers.

"Good day sir, is Tahira in?"

"Yes, she is. Hold on, let me go call her."

A few minutes later Tahira comes on the phone. "Who is this?"

"Your husband," Tavario states calmly.

"I have no husband."

"Woman, what is your problem? I called so that we can talk. I haven't seen you in months, the least you can do is talk to me."

"Why? Where's your **son**?"

"The boy's not my son."

"There's no proof of that," Tahira fumes. "Mr. Mikos, what do you want?"

"You, Mrs. Mikos. I want you home, with me."

"I'm a Zagori. I no longer want to be associated with the Mikos name."

"Tell that to Jesus," Tavario advises. "Unless one of us dies, you're stuck with me."

Tahira sighs heavily. "Why did you call me?"

"I'm coming to bring you home. We can go to counseling. I'll do whatever it takes to win your heart back."

"Forget all that," she scoffs. "Save your money. Don't waste my time. You can't erase a child. You **lied** to me when you said you had no children."

"How was I supposed to know whether or not I fathered a child with a woman who I hadn't spoken to in years? She never told me anything and seven years later she shows up? Does that make sense to you?"

"I really don't care about your rationalization. Stop bothering me. Don't call this house again. You're disturbing my family."

"You are my family and in my prayers, Empress."

"You think this is a joke, Tavario? We'll see what's funny when you receive the divorce papers." With that Tahira ends the call.

After hanging up the phone, Tahira washes her face from the tears. She plops down on her bed, scrolling through her messages. The phone vibrates in her hand and she clicks to accept the video call.

"I haven't received your response to walk in the wedding," Olympia states frantically. "Are you two coming?"

Olympia Gáïos, Greek native and Agent in the NIU was Tahira's close friend for over five years. Though they'd met under dreadful circumstances, Olympia proved to be a true friend. When she and Tavario honeymooned in Greece, they visited Olympia and Xylon.

"To be honest, I may be the only one walking," Tahira announces nonchalantly.

"You still haven't spoken to him?"

"We've spoken, but nothing has changed."

"Is he even trying?" Olympia prods.

"It's Tavario we're speaking about, of course he's trying. But, it doesn't change the dire situation we're in. The petition for divorce has already been sent out."

"I can't believe you're seriously divorcing the man you wanted to marry for twenty years over an accusation. Besides that, has he mistreated you in anyway?"

"No he hasn't. He's been nothing but kind, loving, and supportive. Everything he's vowed to do."

"Tahira, you know I love you right?"

"I hear a **but** coming."

"You're **stubborn**," Olympia chides. "You got a gem of a husband who'd do anything for you and you're willingly throwing him into the arms of another woman? He didn't cheat on you. If the boy turns out to be his son, then do what other women do, help raise the child."

"Would you do that if you found out Xylon fathered another woman's baby?"

"If it didn't happen during the time we got together then **yes**. I love him."

"It's easy to say yes when you're not going through it. The issue isn't the boy."

"Then what is?"

"The fact that I can't give my husband the gift of fatherhood," Tahira sobs.

"Oh sweetie, I wish I can hug you right now. Your face is puffing up."

"Can we end this video call?"

"You wish," Olympia laughs. "Back to my request, will you be able to make it?"

"I'll think about it. It's still a few months away," Tahira responds, wiping the tears from her eyes.

"December is right around the corner."

"The Greeks love their big weddings."

"That's tradition. And being the daughter of the leader of the NIU, it's going to be spectacular."

"I'll let you know."

"Tahira, I want you to come here with Tavario."

"Can't make that promise."

"He'll be here. I know it."

"Whatever you say Ms. Gáïos, soon to be Mrs. Yarbrough."

"Has a nice ring to it doesn't it? Olympia Yarbrough. Mr. and Mrs. Xylon Yarbrough. God is so amazing."

"Indeed. Good night girlie."

Chapter

13

57 Not So Happily Ever After

IN THE CIRCUIT COURT OF THE 4TH
JUDICIAL CIRCUIT IN AND FOR
SAHELUNA, LUX POINT MILANO

FAMILY DIVISION
CASE NO: 89_14702PD5

IN RE: THE MARRIAGE OF
TAHIRA I.A. ZAGORI
Petitioner-Wife,

PETITION FOR DISSOLUTION
OF MARRIAGE

and

TAVARIO E. MIKOS
Respondent-Husband,

For her Petition for Dissolution of Marriage, the Wife States:

DISSOLUTION OF MARRIAGE: This is an action of dissolution of marriage, which is being filed only after Petitioner has attempted to redeem the marriage of the parties. However, "Tavario" has an illegitimate son who the wife had no prior knowledge of and has left her with no choice but to divorce him.

RESIDENCY: Both parties have been residents of the State of *Saheluna* for more than four months prior to the filing date of this petition.

MARRIAGE: The parties were married on January 20, 2023, in *Jozelle Oasis, Fortazonio.*

IRRETRIEVABLY BROKEN: The marriage of the parties is irretrievably broken because of the Husband's negligence, disregard for his wife's feelings, emotional trauma, and the above mentioned illegitimate child.

Hours passed since Tavario received the petition of divorce from his wife. It was the single most absurd thing she'd ever done. Moving away was one thing, but expecting him to sign divorce papers when he hadn't done anything wrong was ludicrous.

He tried to get a flight to Fortazonio that very night, but the flights were all booked until the following week. Instead of using his prior status as a movie star to get on a flight or even choosing standby, he decided to use the extra days to pray and strategize. One way or the other this situation would be resolved before the month ended. He got down on his knees to pray…

> "Dear Lord, I leave it all in Your hands. Vindicate my cause Jesus. Tahira is Your daughter and You know more than I do how to deal with this situation. Thank You for giving me peace and assurance that it will work out. In Jesus' name, Amen."

Chapter

14

*T*ahira had been in Fortazonio for four days and it felt like an eternity since she'd left her matrimonial home. However, there was no turning back. That night she went with her mother to a women's conference.

"We're happy to have our very own daughter, Tahira Mikos in our midst. Welcome home," Minister Ankara Hizaor announces.

Minister Hizaor was a dynamic woman of God. She, along with her husband Pastor Nakoa Hizaor, worked incredulously to not only win souls for God's kingdom, but to disciple and train them to be effective servants fulfilling the Great Commission.

Tahira is greeted by those around her, while others cheer excitedly.

"Sis. Mikos, do you have a word for us?" Ankara inquires.

Tahira stands nervously and greets the women. "Greetings sisters, it is good to be in the house of the Lord, fellowshipping with you all tonight."

"Thank you my sister," Minister Hizaor smiles before beginning her message. "Tonight we're going to speak about **Taming the Tongue**. Let us pray."

"Hmmmm," Tahiti says loudly, eyeing her daughter.

Tahira begins to squirm, feeling a heavy conviction about to come on.

"Turn with me to Proverbs 18:21, King James Version." Ankara observes the audience and speaks with authority. Her God given calling was apparent. *"'Death and life are in the power of the tongue: and they that love it shall eat the fruit thereof.'* Now this is a verse that many of us use so much that it has become cliché. Do we understand what the writer is saying? The magnitude of our words? What we put into the atmosphere? So many times we go around uttering words in a nonchalant manner not thinking about the repercussions of our speech. We use phrases sometimes jokingly, other times innocently, but it holds a lot of weight in the spiritual realm.

We have an enemy whose number one goal is to *steal, kill, and destroy* God's people. Yet we say things haphazardly. One example: a mother telling her child **'you'll be the death of me.'** Seems simple enough, but keep saying it and it just may happen. Or what about the infamous line **'you're just like your father.'** If the speaker was referring to God the Father in Heaven then it won't be an issue, but most of the times they're referring to a no good man.

> Philippians 4:8 says, *'Finally, brethren, whatsoever things are true, whatsoever things are honest, whatsoever things are just, whatsoever things are pure, whatsoever things are lovely, whatsoever things are of good report; if there be any virtue, and if there be any praise, think on these things.'*

Let us stop using the word of God as a mere book and truly apply what we read and hear. Let us not only be *hearers* of the word, but *doers* also...

As my sermon comes to a close there is someone in our congregation today who is going through a life or death situation. Not in the traditional sense, but dissolution of a covenant that God ordained."

Feeling uneasy in her seat, Tahira makes her way to the altar and throws herself on the ground, crying hysterically.

Ankara kneels next to Tahira and hugs her. Tahiti and the other women in the congregation also join them, standing in agreement.

"Now ladies, as stated before, Tahira is one of our own. When one part of the body is hurting it affects us all. Let us spend the rest of this session praying for our dear sister…"

At the end of the session the congregation is dismissed. "Ladies before you go," Ankara states, "don't forget that tomorrow night we have Prophetess Jiyuan Tkachenko ministering the word. Please come early and bring a friend. It's going to be a powerful night of deliverance."

Chapter

15

64 *Not So Happily Ever After*

*T*he following morning, Tavario runs to answer the door. He looks on the video monitor. The last thing he needed was for his life to become a public spectacle. However, he knew that the woman would be relentless. Before opening the door, he utters a word of prayer.

"Haselt, meet your daddy, Tavario Mikos," Nova declares when the door is opened.

"He's not my daddy," the boy cries, hiding behind his mother. "I want my real daddy."

"Pay him no mind," Nova smiles at Tavario. "He's shy. Are you going to let us in?"

Tavario closes the door behind him. "No, we can go to the park down the road."

"Suit yourself. Haselt, would you like to go to the park?"

"NO!" he pouts loudly.

Tavario sighs. *Father HELP!*

At the park, while Nova and Tavario sits on a bench, Haselt chases birds on the ground.

"He's such an energetic boy, just like his father," Nova blushes.

"Boys are energetic in general. Please don't refer to me as his **father**, when we don't know for sure."

"Why would I lie about his paternity?"

"Why'd you wait so long to tell me?"

"I was embarrassed," Nova reveals. "Being a model and pregnant isn't ideal. It's frowned upon. I was on top of my game, so my publicist suggested I go away and hide the pregnancy."

"The timing doesn't add up."

"Are you trying to tell me I don't know when I conceived my son?"

"I don't doubt you know the timeframe, but I know for a fact that it wasn't with me."

"You're trying to embarrass me yet again. I know that you're his father."

"Then prove it with a DNA test."

"I don't need it."

Tavario stares at Nova. "I'm no fool. I know of too many men in the industry who've fallen prey to this type of scheme before."

"This isn't a scheme. He is **our** son."

"If you were concerned about him, you'd allow for the test to take place to alleviate all doubts. If he is mine, I will gladly take care of him."

Nova's eyes glisten. "Then does that mean you will divorce Tahira?"

"That has not and will never be an option," Tavario answers. "I love my wife."

"Does she love you?"

"What exactly did you think introducing me to Haselt would do? You thought I'd divorce my wife so that the three of us would become one big happy family?"

"That's exactly what I expect," Nova nods. "You knew me way before her, **inside** and **out**."

"Nova STOP! I married Tahira and I love her. I don't love you."

"You did at one point."

"I thought I did, but we were young. I didn't know what love was until Jesus, and Tahira."

"Oh come off that. Tahira. Tahira. I'm tired of hearing about that **commoner**."

"She's no commoner I can tell you that. She is and will forever be Mrs. Tavario E. Mikos."

"Why are you defending a woman who isn't even here? You sound pathetic."

"Your opinions don't matter."

"You really have changed," she pauses, "into a **weak** man."

"I may be weak by human standards, but I serve a great and powerful God. The only God. Let HIM work in your life. Help you deal with your past. Trying to force me to divorce my wife isn't going to erase the emptiness you feel inside. I mean what other reason would you have to try and break up someone's marriage for your own gain?"

"You know what? I've HAD ENOUGH! I'm leaving. If you're not going to take care of your son the nice way then I'll have to take matters into my own hands." She stands up and calls out to her son, "Haselt, let's go. Your daddy is disrespecting mommy."

Chapter

16

Saturday Night

"*I* am pleased to welcome a true woman of God in our midst. My best friend of over twenty-five years, Prophetess Jiyuan Tkachenko. Let's give her a round of applause as she comes," Minister Hizaor proclaims.

Tahira joins her mother and the other women of *Fortazonio House of Worship* in welcoming the guest speaker.

Twenty minutes after her sermonette, the Prophetess asks everyone to stand. The worship team begins to sing a soft melody of praise unto Jesus.

"Yes Lord," Jiyuan utters. "Tonight is going to be a night of **Exposing the Deceiver**."

Immediately a woman began wailing in the back row.

"Some of you in here are suffering great pain at the hands of others. Then there are those of you who have been deceived into believing a lie. Everyone lift your hands and begin to cry out to God on behalf of the woman next to you. You may or may not know what she's going through, but breakthrough is about to take place. Healing is about to take place. Worship team continue singing. All over this room cry out to Jesus," Jiyuan encourages.

The sound of the women wailing, reminded Tahira of the time she went to Brazil and heard the people from a church in São Paulo crying out to God.

"The woman who is going through an issue with her wayward children, please step forward. You've been dealing with this

situation for two years and no one knows. God wants you to take your rightful place as the leader of your household. Your

husband died three years ago, leaving you with two rebellious teenagers. You've skipped out on church many times for fear

of being rejected. This isn't your home church, but someone invited you. I want you and the woman who invited you to come to the altar," Prophetess Tkachenko calls out.

When Tahira opens her eyes, she observes two visitors walking. One of the women begins to bawl in agony. The one Tahira guesses is a widow.

Jiyuan looks at both women. "Lift your hands," she commands. The women lift their hands. "God has placed this woman in your life as a mother. You didn't grow up knowing your mother. And although she started off as a co-worker, you both became close, like mother-daughter. She's crying because she's always wanted a daughter, but was never able to conceive..."

At that moment Tahira wipes tears from her eyes, relating to the older of the two women.

This woman had infertility issues?

"You are her daughter," the Prophetess reveals. "She may not have given birth to you, but you're mother and daughter; like Naomi and Ruth."

71 *Not So Happily Ever After*

The women cry even louder.

Jiyuan looks at the older woman. "Your daughter needs you to help her with her children. It won't be forever, and I don't mean physically, even though that is necessary. But spiritually; you need to travail for her. God is going to deal with those children. HE needs you to pray for her because she is going to be one of many. You will be a mother of nations."

"Oh Jesus, I thank You," the older woman cries out.

Without missing a beat, Jiyuan scans the audience. "The woman who's hiding in the back wearing a pink dress, please come forward."

The woman walks shyly to the front.

"Place your right hand on your left ring finger." She follows the instructions. "You will be married by this time next year. The man who you've rejected in your heart and pray against every night **IS** your husband. Stop running from him. He loves you. He may not be your ideal, but he's the one God has for you because of what HE has called you both to do. He's going to call you tonight and ask you out. In his mind this'll be the **final** attempt because oh has he tried. Be obedient, say yes to him."

Rubbing the tears from her eyes the shy woman returns to her seat.

Moments later, Jiyuan steps in front of a young woman around the age of 21. "Let him go. He's a deceiver. He came into your life at your low point and has sweet talked his way into your heart and your bed. LET. HIM. GO. TONIGHT. If you don't, he will **KILL** you."

The young woman drops on the floor and cries in pain. Two ushers go to pray for her.

"Finally, the woman aged 29 whose initials are TM please step forward."

She can't be serious.

"Hurry, we don't have all night. Yes, I know you're afraid of your business being exposed, but God is going to work things out."

"Go sweetie," Tahiti gently pushes Tahira into the aisle.

"Mom you come too. Your daughter trusts you. Hold her hand."

Tahiti does as the Prophetess commands.

Jiyuan looks at Tahira sternly. "Your situation is partially as a result of your **mouth** and your unwillingness to wait on God."

The tears begin to fall down Tahira's cheeks.

"Repent of your words. Every word that you spoke against your husband, your marriage, and future, I **REBUKE** it in Jesus' name. I see double blessing in your future. I don't know what that means to you, but I see the number two. The person who is trying to destroy your marriage is a deceiver and will be exposed **publicly**. God will vindicate you, your husband, and your legacy..."

When the service ends Tahira is still seen crying on the altar. Her mother calls for her to go home.

73 *Not So Happily Ever After*

Jiyuan stops her. "Let her finish. Mom, you're going to need to pray now more than ever for your daughter because it's going to get worse before it gets better. I know she's not strong enough to hear that, but you need to be strong for her. All will be revealed before this month ends."

Chapter

17

75 Not So Happily Ever After

*A*lthough Tahira had no idea what the number two signified in the prophecy, she hoped it had to do with the timeframe of her pregnancy. In two months or worst case scenario, two years. One thing she knew for sure, she had to work on controlling her mouth.

"KNOCK! KNOCK!"

"Who is it?" Tahira calls out.

"It's me."

"Come in, mom."

"Sweetie, are you alright?" Tahiti sits on the bed. "I know last night's service had you thinking about your future."

"You can say it; it had me thinking about my **mouth**."

"What is your next step?"

"Honestly, I don't know. One part of me wants to call Tavario and make up, but the other can't get over what is happening in our marriage. I've already sent out the divorce papers. It can't be undone."

"Of course you can revoke the petition. This is your marriage. Although it's a law binding contract on earth, it's God ordained."

Tahira sighs.

"Do you love him?"

"Yes, I do."

"Then fight for your marriage. No matter the outcome, you can handle it together because God is at the center of your marriage. Don't forget that part."

"A child with another woman, though? WHY is this happening?"

Tahiti comforts her daughter. "I don't have the answers, but God does."

"I need to do something, if you'll excuse me for a bit. I'll be down soon to help you with breakfast."

"That's ok. I can handle it. You have a lot on your mind. Finish up here and then join us." Tahiti exits the room.

"You can do this Tahira, you can do this."

Picking up the home pregnancy test, Tahira goes to the bathroom.

Minutes later she goes in to check on the results.

NOT PREGNANT.

She sits on the bathroom floor and wails.

Chapter

18

78 *Not So Happily Ever After*

Monday

*T*avario nervously rings the Zagori doorbell. He felt like a teenager going on a date for the first time, instead of a husband going to win back his wife.

"Come in. Come in," Ramiro greets. "Tahira's upstairs."

Tavario gives his father-in-law a hug. "How's she doing?"

"You have to ask her. I haven't experienced this type of behavior since her adolescent years."

Tavario sighs. "This is all my fault."

"Don't blame yourself. She has a part to play. This foolishness has gone on for far too long."

"Ra—" Tahiti stops when she sees her son-in-law. "You came. It's about time. Go get your wife. She's been miserable without you."

Tahira wipes the sleep out her eyes when she hears the knock.

"Mom, I'm—" Before she finishes her statement, the door opens and her husband stood with the world's most pitiful look on his face. "Uggh! What are you doing here?" she scoffs.

79 *Not So Happily Ever After*

"I came for us to talk," Tavario walks over to her bed. "I did tell you I was coming."

"Whoop de doo," Tahira laughs sarcastically. "I don't want to be around you."

"When are you coming home? I miss you. I miss us. I've been lonely without you."

"Don't you have a **son** to bring you joy?"

"I don't know if he's my son. No test has been done to prove otherwise."

"Why are you here? You come in my hometown to rub it in my face even more? At least let me have my dignity. Please stay away from me."

"Tahira, is this what you really want?" he strokes her hand, but she pulls away.

"Did you get the petition?"

"Yes."

"And?"

"I threw it away," Tavario states.

"You're really prolonging the inevitable."

"I'm not prolonging anything. I'm not signing, nor will I ever sign any papers designed to separate me from the only woman I love."

"Tell that to Nova."

"She has nothing to do with our marriage."

"But, she has everything to do with you being a father."

"No one knows for sure. She doesn't even seem to know. I'm going to get to the bottom of this."

"Why are you staring at me like that?"

"You're beautiful."

Tahira tries to hide the blush forming on her cheeks.

"Awwww. I got a blush."

"So?" Tahira snaps back to reality. "That doesn't mean anything. Why don't you go back to your country? Don't you have work?"

"Nothing is more important than you."

She mockingly claps. "And the award for most dramatic goes to... You guessed it, Tavario Mikos."

"You can push me away all you want. I'm staying. Hire all the lawyers on the planet. I'm staying here, Tahira Inielle Aiyoki Mikos. Do you hear me? I love you and will do whatever it takes to win you back."

"I wish my parents didn't like you or else you wouldn't be in here right now."

Tahira's mother calls them for lunch.

"Are you hungry? Let's go," Tavario encourages.

"I don't want any food."

"Are you going to come willingly? Or am I going to have to hold your hand?"

Tahira couldn't help but laugh at his statement, remembering the time she officially met the Mikos' while they stayed at *Holbrook Resort & Spa.*

This doesn't mean anything though. I'm still going through with the divorce no matter what he tries...

Chapter

19

83 *Not So Happily Ever After*

After lunch, the family gathered to watch a movie. Just then a news bulletin comes across the screen.

> "28 year old Vias Supermodel, Nova Duesing has been on a tirade of sorts accusing former actor Tavario Mikos of being a deadbeat father to their 7 year old son, Haselt Duesing. Nova, who hid her pregnancy from the limelight, has been raising her son in secrecy according to her Rep. As you can see from the video footage, the trio were spotted having a quiet family day at the park. However, things turned ugly after Nova asked Tavario to step up to the plate. Tavario has denied being the boy's father. No comment has been made from Tavario or his Rep. And now, back to your regularly scheduled program..."

Tahira looks at her husband. "When did you spend time with that woman and her son?" she asked in muted sobs. "Or should I say **your** son."

"It's not what it looks like," Tavario replies.

"Oh, don't you even TRY IT. Not only have you humiliated me in private, but PUBLIC AS WELL? HAVE YOU NO SHAME? Now I can have no peace in my hometown. Everyone's going to be staring and laughing at me."

Tavario tries to take his wife's hand and she slaps him.

"DON'T YOU DARE TOUCH ME YOU LIAR. YOU SAID NOTHING WAS GOING ON BETWEEN YOU TWO. NOW THERE'S VIDEO FOOTAGE OF YOUR LITTLE OUTING? Do you care about me at all?" Tahira laments.

"Of course I do. I love you."

"You see mom, dad... Do you see what this man is putting me through? Is this the life you want for your daughter?"

"Tahira please let him explain."

"Really dad, you're not even going to defend me? You're defending **him**?"

"Listen to your father," Tahiti adds.

"I can't believe you both right now." Tahira turns her gaze back to Tavario. "This is what you wanted; to make me out to be the **fool** of Fortazonio?"

"Empress, I don't want any of this. I'm going to fix it," Tavario cries.

"Forget it. There's nothing to fix. You'd better meet me in that lawyer's office tomorrow or I am going to put a restraining order out against you. I don't want you near me. LEAVE THIS HOUSE RIGHT NOW. Make him leave or I AM LEAVING."

"Sweetie, this isn't necessary," her father responds.

"I'm serious. If he doesn't leave, I'm leaving and I'm going to have nothing to do with any of you."

Tahiti pulls Tahira out to the foyer. "Honey, do you remember what the Prophetess said? *'God will vindicate you, your husband and your legacy.'* What you didn't hear is what she said to me after, *'...it's going to get worse before it gets better...However, all will be revealed before this month ends.'* So please, don't do this."

Tahira looks her mother in the eye. "YOU KNEW THIS WAS GOING TO HAPPEN?"

"Don't raise your voice at me."

"Unreal!" Tahira storms off in anguish.

Minutes later, Tahira drags her suitcase down the stairs, staring at her parents and soon to be ex-husband. "Since you're **best** friends of sorts, I'm going to leave you all here to sing happy songs with one another. None of you actually care about me. Tavario, you'd better be in that office tomorrow or you will hate me for what I will do next—"

Chapter

20

87 Not So Happily Ever After

"*T*hank you Mr. Islington for meeting with us this morning."

"Mrs. Mikos, what seems to be the problem?" the lawyer prods.

"Call me Tahira. I don't want **any** association with that last name."

Mr. Islington turns to Tavario. "Mr. Mikos, can you explain to me why we're here today?"

Tavario glances at his wife. "You'll have to ask her."

The lawyer walks to his chair and sits down in front of the couple, "Tahira?"

"Well Mr. Islington, I've sent my husband divorce papers to which he informed me that he and I quote *'threw it away'*. Mr. Mikos' REFUSAL to sign the papers has put me in a position to take drastic measures."

"I see." He looks at Tavario, noting his stance. "Would you like to add anything?"

"No," Tavario retorts.

The lawyer returns his gaze to Tahira.

"Ask him about his son," Tahira scoffs.

Mr. Islington looks at Tavario.

"I can't comment on what I don't know. A woman from my past returned a few months ago, claiming that I fathered her seven year old son. She has refused to allow me to take a DNA test to prove the paternity."

"Tahira, is this why you want a divorce?"

"It's part of the issue," Tahira mumbles to the lawyer.

"While it goes against my job description, I can see that you two love one another," Mr. Islington observes. "Even though Mrs. Mikos—"

"Ms. **Zagori**." Tahira corrects.

Mr. Islington gives her a stern warning and continues his speech, "Mrs. Mikos is trying to put on a façade. Have you two tried counseling?"

"What kind of divorce lawyer are you?" Tahira replies, rolling her eyes.

"Usually the couples who come into my office are bent on divorcing. They can't even look at, not to mention sit next to each other. But, Mrs. Mikos I can see that you love your husband. Every time he speaks, your body language is a giveaway. Divorce is ugly. Are you sure you want to go through with these proceedings?"

"I-I..." Before she could continue her rant, Tahira vomits.

Chapter

_21_

*F*orty minutes later, Tavario bursts through the ER door. "Can I please see my wife?" he asks the nurse.

"I'm sorry, and you are?"

Tavario stares at the nurse, annoyed. "Tavario Mikos. My wife is in there."

"Can I see some ID?"

"Lady come on, you know who I am."

"Excuse me?" the nurse scoffs. "Hospital policy, I need to see some ID."

Tavario slams his ID on the counter.

"I'm sorry Mr. Mikos; your wife has stated that she doesn't want you in her room."

"What is the issue?"

"I can't divulge that information to you," the nurse apologizes, "Next of kin only."

"I'm her **husband**."

"I understand, but we must respect the patient's wishes in these circumstances."

"This is ridiculous," Tavario snaps.

"Can you please step aside, so that I can speak to the gentleman behind you?"

Tahiti storms through the hospital. "Where is she? Where is my baby girl?"

"Oh good, you made it," Tavario greets.

His mother-in-law looks at him. "Why aren't you inside?"

"The nurse said that Tahira doesn't want me in there," Tavario shrugs.

"I'll go speak to her." Ramiro walks over to the nurse's station.

"Tavario, what happened?"

"I don't know," he replies. "One minute the divorce lawyer was asking her some questions, the next she threw up and passed out."

Tahiti paces the hall. "This situation is absurd."

Ramiro returns from the nurse's station. "I've spoken to the nurse and she's stated that you can see Tahira as long as one
of us is in the room."

Tavario exhales. "Thank you, sir."

"Let's go," Ramiro leads.

2 Hours Later

"Where are my parents?"

"They went home to rest until tomorrow," Tavario informs.

"You're not supposed to be in here." Tahira notes, grimacing.

"Lay down *Dolcezza*. It's okay. I'm not going anywhere."

"I don't want you here. I gave the doctor specific instructions."

"Did he say what was wrong?"

"That's none of your business," she gruffly replies.

"I wouldn't be here if I didn't care."

"Possible symptoms of PCOS."

"You mean the illness you don't have?"

"Everyone can't be wrong, Tavario."

"But, you used the word **possible**. Are you saying he isn't sure?"

"No one has actually told me anything. They're still running tests."

"So you're diagnosing yourself?" he asks.

"Can you leave? You're not welcomed here."

"I'm not going anywhere."

Tahira presses the call bell.

Moments later her nurse enters. "Ms. Zagori, you rang?"

"Yes, this man is disturbing my peace and I would like him out of my room."

"Sir, I've informed you of Ms. Zagori's request. You need to leave before I call security."

Tavario shakes his head. "Ms. Zagori? Tahira are you kicking me out?"

"Nurse!" Tahira pleads.

"Sir, please..." the nurse appeals.

Chapter

22

95 *Not So Happily Ever After*

*T*ahira's world came crashing down five minutes later, when Nova walks into her hospital room. "Well, well, well, if it isn't the wannabee Mrs. Mikos."

Tahira squirms in her bed trying not to pull out her IV. "Who allowed you in my room?"

"Don't worry. I told them that I'm a friend. I brought Haselt to meet you."

"Mommy, can I go get a soda from the vending machine?"

"We've spoken about this already. No sodas," Nova replies.

"But mommyyyyyyyy—" Haselt whines.

"Here's some money to get a snack, but NO soda. I'm going to know if you do."

"I know you have eyes everywhere."

"Yes, that's right. Hurry back."

"Okay." Haselt runs out of the room.

"Such a sweet boy. I wish his daddy would think so and help take care of him." Nova says. She pulls a chair to Tahira's bedside.

"Nova, I don't have the energy for this. Why are you here? You won. Did you come to gloat? Did you come in my hometown to disturb the peace? You made a public declaration about my husband's alleged negligence. Now here you are in my hospital room. How did you know I was here?"

"I have my ways of finding things out. Where is my son's father by the way?"

"I don't know where Tavario is. I do know I don't want you in my room. I'm trying to rest."

"Why are you trying to keep him away from his son?"

"Why aren't you allowing him to take a DNA test?" Tahira counters.

"That's none of your business," Nova snaps. You don't deserve him. I'm supposed to be Mrs. Tavario Mikos, not you."

"Yet here we are. I have the ring. Leave my husband and marriage alone."

"I was there for him when he was in his early stages of adulthood. Helped shape him into the man he is today. You don't deserve the fruits of **my labor**!"

"Do you hear yourself when you talk? You sound deluded. What you and **my** husband had was ages ago. *Ancient history!*
If Haselt is his son, Tavario will do right by him. But, if he isn't you need to leave him alone. You're embarrassing yourself; using that poor little boy to justify your delusions of grandeur."

"Don't talk about my son," Nova retorts angrily.

"Isn't that why you're here? To try and coerce your way into my husband's heart to take care of a child he didn't father?"

"HOW DARE YOU!"

"I've had enough of you Nova. Get out of my hospital room before I call security."

"I'm not going anywhere without Tavario," Nova contends.

"He doesn't want you. You're pathetic."

Nova laughs. "What can you do for him? You're a **barren** woman."

The words permeated Tahira's soul. Tears began to fall.

She is right...

Chapter

23

99 *Not So Happily Ever After*

*H*aselt enters the room. "Mommy, look, I found daddy outside."

"Yes my son. Aren't you happy to see him?" Nova beams.

Tahira sniffles as the tears continued to fall.

Over one year we've been trying and nothing. In comes Insta-Nova with Haselt. SIGH! When will this humiliation end?

"Nova, why are you here?" Tavario sighs with irritation. "How did you know where to find me?"

"I have my ways. Besides I was in the neighborhood. My son said he wanted to see his daddy so I made it happen. Sacrifices..." she shrugs.

"You're going overboard with this. Stop disrespecting me and my wife."

"Haselt is your son and I'd do anything for his happiness. That's what a real **mother** does." Nova blurts, obviously throwing punches at Tahira's inability to conceive.

"You need to leave," Tahira declares.

"I have no problem. Tavario, I'll be on your tail until you pay me the child support money."

"Mommy, can we get ice-cream?"

"Yes and next time daddy will go with us. But, he needs to speak to this lady right now."

Haselt smiles and exits the room with Nova.

"I'm sorry that she showed up. We're going to get through this."

Tahira glares ferociously at her husband. "I was speaking to you also. You need to **leave**. NOW TAVARIO. LEAVE!"

Chapter

24

"*D*o you need me to get anything for you?" Tahiti asks her daughter later that night.

Tahira was released from the hospital and given medication for pain.

"No thanks mom, I'm fine." Tahira replies, putting down a cup on her nightstand. "Is that man still here?"

Tahiti sits on the bed. "That **man** is your husband. Why don't you talk to him?"

"He's the reason that I ended up in the hospital in the first place."

"No, he's not."

"There you go defending him again. I'm your child, not Tavario."

"He's my son-in-law," Tahiti says. "I love him and you will work this out."

"There's nothing to work out. Can you believe Nova brought her son to the hospital? Why are they torturing me?"

"You need to ask the Lord how to deal with this. You're fighting the wrong enemy. Your husband is not the enemy."

"That's easy for you to say. You never had to deal with another woman using a child to destroy your marriage."

"If Haselt is Tavario's son, you will deal with it like mature adults. That boy did not ask to be in this position."

"They can go be a family for all I care."

"You do care. Stop lying to yourself."

"I need to rest. Don't worry; I will be out of your hair soon. When I feel strong enough to fly, I'm leaving."

Tahiti pushes a strand of hair from Tahira's face. "Do you remember when you found out about Cadell? Do you remember the downward spiral that your life took?"

"Where's this going?"

"All that happened to you, but you concluded that God protected you through it all. HE is the same God."

"I'm not doubting God."

"Really? Because that's exactly what you're doing. You got specific instructions about your situation. Pray Tahira. Fast even. This is your battle to fight. I can't fight for your marriage for you."

"STOPPPPPPPP! You're confusing me. I've already made up my mind. I'm divorcing Tavario. There's nothing that anyone can do about it."

"You're being stubborn." Tahiti gets up and opens the door. "All I know is that you made marriage vows and now that the *worst* has happened, you're giving up. Marriage is for mature adults. If you want to be a baby, that's on you. Whatever happens from here on out is your call. That man loves you, but if you keep pushing him away..." With that her mother slams the door.

Rolling her eyes at her mother's attempts, Tahira dials her best friend.

"How are you feeling?"

"I'm okay. My marital issues have escalated since that woman showed up in my hospital room."

"They need to beef up security," Kaiora adds. "It's bad that they allow anyone to walk in there."

"That's not the point. I want to know her motive for coming."

"Girl, forget about her. You need to conserve your energy."

"F-Forget about her? The woman is **everywhere**. She has publicly humiliated me and my husband."

"So he's *still* your husband?"

"Not for long."

"Still going through with the divorce?"

"Yes!" Tahira stresses.

"Calm down," Kaiora replies.

"I need my rest. I'll call you tomorrow."

"Wait a minute girl—"

Tahira hangs up the phone and begins to cry.

"Eat Tavario," Tahiti commands, placing a bowl of *Quayap Soup* in front of him.

"Not hungry."

"Son, starving yourself isn't going to resolve anything."

"Then what is? I'm losing it. She hasn't said a word to me since we left the hospital. That was five hours ago."

"You're a man of prayer. Keep praying and believing God."

"**Nothing** is happening Ms. Tahiti."

"You know that's not true. We like to quote the verses about holding on to our faith and fighting the good fight, but when it gets down to it... We cower under pressure."

"Have you and Mr. Z ever had any marital issues?"

"What couple doesn't? However, we learned to weather our storms and trust God."

"Come on, that's not what I need now. No **cutesified** version
of Christianity. Share please, a time where you had to fight for your marriage."

Tahiti looks at him. "Okay, but promise me you won't share it with anyone..."

Chapter

25

107 *Not So Happily Ever After*

" *T*ahira. Tahira. I need your help," a man calls out into the abyss.

Tahira looks up at the man in astonishment.

No. It can't be.

"You're not supposed to be here. This isn't real."

"Tahira, please help me," he continues.

"Cadell, when did you get out of prison?"

"Let's not speak about that here. Can we go somewhere and talk?"

"I'm not going anywhere with you. You're supposed to be in prison," she shrieks.

"And yet, here I am."

"What do you want? Please don't hurt me."

"I'd never hurt you Tahira. I don't want to make a scene."

"Stay away from me."

"I need your help."

"NO!"

"Please Tahira."

Covering her ears she begins to shake. "No. No. You're not real. You're not here. I'm not seeing you. This is a dream."

"Why are you ignoring me?" Cadell continues, "You're the only one who can help me."

"Stop talking. You're a lying murderer. Stay away from me."

"Please Tahira."

"Cadell, leave me alone."

"I need your help," he pleads, reaching out to her.

"DON'T TOUCH ME."

"Tahira? Tahira. Wake up."

"I said don't touch me, Cadell!"

"Cadell?"

Rubbing her eyes, Tahira wakes up from her nightmare. "Oh, it's you. Why are you still here?"

"I heard you screaming so I came to check on you."

She sits up and pulls the covers to her chin. "I'm fine. You didn't have to come."

"I'm your husband."

"Not for long."

"Were you having a dream about your ex?"

"What are you talking about?"

"I heard you screaming his name. Why were you dreaming about your ex? Do you still have feelings for him?"

"There's nothing to discuss. He's the past."

"Tahira, is there something you're not telling me?"

"It was a **dream**. I don't know why he came in my dream."

"Maybe you're subconsciously thinking about him."

"I haven't seen Cadell in years. I don't think about him. He's in prison. But, you've got some nerve to ask me about my ex who I **dreamed** about, yet your ex is parading around your possible son. There's no discussion here. You're winning this humiliation competition."

"Is that what you think I'm trying to do, humiliate you? I didn't know anything about Haselt."

"Don't. Don't call his name. Please. It hurts."

Tavario motions toward his wife.

"Stay where you are. I'm fine."

"*Dolcezza*, please. Let's talk about this."

"I don't want to talk about anything. You're a liar and you've kept this secret from me."

"I didn't know about it."

"But, you did sleep with her didn't you?"

Tavario sighs in angst. "That was months before I met you."

"You never told me what happened when she visited Ruvenivi for her photoshoot. Do you remember that time you two left me on the beach?"

"Nothing happened."

"Maybe you should go back to being an actor because you're really good at pretending."

"I'm trying to do the right thing, but you're not making this easy for me."

"It's **always** about you. You haven't considered ONCE how I feel. This is humiliating. I'm a joke in my own country, Starr Islands, and the entire world. Everyone knows about this situation YOU CREATED. Let it remain about you because I'm DONE!"

"STOP IT TAHIRA," Tavario yells.

Tahira jumps out of the bed and puts on her robe. "Did you just scream at me?"

"Why are you fighting against me? We should be handling this together."

"Tavario you just yelled at me? You've never raised your voice at me before."

"You've been raising your voice this entire time."

"There we go competing again. I don't want to do this with you anymore. Pack your bags, LEAVE MY PARENTS' HOUSE AND GO TO YOUR FAMILY. I'M DONE." Tahira takes her wedding ring from the drawer and throws it on the floor in front of him. "You can pawn it or whatever. Use the money to help pay for Haselt's child support. Just GET OUT OF HERE," she utters, slamming the door behind her.

"My son, where are you going?" Tahiti asks Tavario when he arrived in the kitchen.

"Back home."

"What happened upstairs? I heard a lot of yelling."

"I love your daughter, believe me, but I can't handle this. I need to go back home."

"Have breakfast. She'll come around. You need to be here with her."

"No, it's toxic. I need to give her space. She has to deal with her issues by herself with God's help. There are times that you have to leave for things to get better. I will fight for us from home. Tahira has to do her part. When we're around one another there's always tension so I'll go for her to think clearly."

"This is not right Tavario, this is not right."

"I know, but that's how it is until Tahira makes her decision."

"I don't want you to get a divorce. You've been through too much together. You just got married."

"*Till death do us part.* That's what I agreed to. Divorce isn't an option. So unless one of us dies, that's the only way..."

Tahiti sighs. "I will continue to pray for the both of you and your marriage."

Tavario hugs Tahiti. "I'll call you when I land. I will check Mr. Z on my way to the airport."

"Is breakfast ready?"

"That's your big question? You're not even going to ask where your husband is."

Tahira shrugs. "Honestly mom, I don't care."

"Yes you do. Stop that!"

"I can order in."

"Right now your marriage is more important than eating." Tahiti begins to rummage through the kitchen drawer. "The nerve
of this girl," she mutters under her breath, as she pulls out the cutlery.

Chapter

26

*H*ours later, Tahiti sat with her husband for lunch. "What are we going to do about her?"

Ramiro takes a bite of his *Winter Salmon*. "I told you to stay out of it."

"We're her parents."

"Tahira is an adult," he answers mid chew. "We've done all that we can for her, but she has to make this step by herself."

"I'm worried. What if they go through with the divorce? I'd never be a grandmother."

"They're not going to get a divorce. Can we just finish lunch?"

"How do you know that?"

"We've been praying and we have to trust God. This is a test for all of us. Our daughter may be weak at the moment, but she will come out of it. It isn't her first time being tested and it won't be the last."

"All of our prayers... are they falling on deaf ears?" Tahiti cries.

Ramiro pulls his wife close and stares into her eyes. "My love, I know that this is painful for you and you want grandchildren, but right now our daughter's well-being and marriage is priority."

She places her head on his shoulder. "You're such a great priest of this household. Strong. Supportive. I'm happy that God chose you to be my husband. I am happy that you chose me to be your wife. I couldn't have prayed for a better husband."

They begin to kiss one another zealously.

Just then, the bell rings.

"Who could that be? We were just getting started," Ramiro chortles, slightly annoyed.

"Go answer the door, we will finish later." Tahiti winks, walking towards the gazebo.

Ramiro opens the door. "Good afternoon Minister Hizaor."

"Elder Ramiro, is Tahira home? I'm sorry to come here unannounced. I felt led to speak with her."

"Of course, come in. She's upstairs in her room."

"Where's the Queen of the house?"

"She's outside."

"I'd like to greet her before I see Tahira."

"Follow me," Ramiro announces.

Chapter

27

117 *Not So Happily Ever After*

A light rap is heard on Tahira's bedroom door. "Good afternoon my daughter, may I come in?"

"Minister Hizaor, sorry I look a mess, I wasn't expecting any guests." Tahira combs her hair with her fingers. "Let me get you a seat."

"Stay. I'll get it." Ankara drags a nearby ottoman.

"To what do I owe this visit?"

"Divine intervention."

Tahira stares at the woman.

Ankara gets straight to the point. "God has been speaking and you're being noncompliant."

"The doctor said I'm supposed to be resting. I hope this isn't a conversation that will add to my stress."

"You're not stressed. All that's happening is a result of your blatant disregard for God's instructions."

"I love and respect you Minister Hizaor, you know that, but please, I'm not in the mood."

"This isn't about moods, child."

"Then what is it about?"

"Your marriage."

"You mean the one on the brink of divorce?"

"The Tahira I know loved her husband, even before he became her husband. This woman sitting in front of me is fighting an unnecessary battle, wounding herself in the process."

"Why is everyone assuming that I don't love my husband? Love isn't the issue here."

"Recite 1 Corinthians 13:4-8 aloud."

"Not now Minister Hizaor. Where are you going with this?"

"Recite."

Tahira sighs and obliges to Ankara's request. "*Love is patient, love is kind. It does not envy, it does not boast, it is not proud. It does not dishonor others, it is not self-seeking, it is not easily angered, it keeps no record of wrongs. Love does not delight in evil but rejoices with the truth. It always protects, always trusts, always hopes, always perseveres. Love never fails. But where there are prophecies, they will cease; where there are tongues, they will be stilled; where there is knowledge, it will pass away.*"

"Do you understand your wedding vows? Did you mean it?"

"Yes, but—"

"When you make a promise like your marriage vows, God holds you accountable to your words. This situation with Nova and Haselt were also included in those vows. So were any other issues that would come up in your marriage."

"You're saying that my marriage had an infidelity clause?"

"This isn't a joke," Ankara replies. "If Nova came and said that Haselt was 1 year old, then that's cause for infidelity claims. But this boy is 7 years old, before you and Tavario started courtship."

"It doesn't make it any easier to deal with."

"This is not a case of an unfaithful husband, this is the past coming to try and ruin your marriage. What are you doing about it?"

"I've already sent out a petition for divorce, which Tavario refuses to sign."

"And he's right not to," Ankara nods in agreement.

"Are you saying that if you were in my situation you'd stay with Pastor Hizaor?"

"Yes I would. The past cannot be erased."

"What if it happened during your marriage?"

"Same answer."

"None of you ladies have ever been humiliated in front of the entire world," Tahira scoffs.

"You're not privy to everyone's story. Stop making assumptions."

"It's easy to state your answers to *what if* scenarios when you're not experiencing it for real."

"I understand hun, believe me. Right now I want you to focus your energy on praying for God to help you. This is what I came here for. Not to argue. Not to go back and forth; but to remind you of the words spoken over your life earlier this month."

"I haven't forgotten. While I tried my best to get out of the situation, my enemy wreaked havoc on my life, embarrassing me."

"What about your husband? Have you considered how it's affecting him?"

"I don't understand."

"You're not the only one who this has or will affect. Tavario has been humiliated too. On top of that, if he possibly fathered this child, it would have been seven years he cannot get back. That's devastating to think his son lived so long without knowing
of his existence. Some fathers are bashed every day for not taking up the mantle, yet Tavario didn't have the opportunity to help raise his son."

"*His son?*" Tahira gasps. "Do you know if Haselt is his son? Did someone tell you?"

Ankara grasps Tahira's hand. "Let's pray. I can see that this conversation is just going to be a circle of accusatory questions and that isn't the purpose of my visit.

Heavenly Father, I come to you in the name of Jesus, thanking You for who You are. Lord You are amazing. You are wonderful. The God of triumph. Of peace. Father You know the beginning from the end. You are truly Alpha and Omega. I thank You for bringing me to Your daughter Tahira today. This situation has gone from a simple statement to a worldwide spectacle and we ask oh Lord that You intervene like never before.

Help her to feel Your goodness in spite of. Help her to know that You haven't given her more than she can bear. Speak to her heart even now Lord Jesus. Hmmmm. Father as that word **deception** has come to my mind I pray that You EXPOSE THE DECEIVER in the name of Jesus. Every man, woman, boy or girl, the enemy has sent to destroy the Mikos' marriage...I rebuke them in Jesus' name. I renounce every curse spoken over their lives, their marriage...

Father... Hmmmm. Her womb. I speak to Tahira's womb right now in Jesus' name. Every lie that the doctor has spoken I rebuke it. Tahira is healed in Your name Jesus. I pray that out of her womb she would bring forth children. Children that would grow up to serve You with their entire being. Father God I pray a double portion. Double anointing for Your daughter's trouble. Wherever Tavario is at this moment, I pray that You will bring him to his knees to cry out before You on behalf of his wife and marriage. I pray a hedge of protection over Tahira's mind right now.

SILENCE the lies. SILENCE the devil in the name of Jesus. I speak **censorship** over Tahira's thoughts and mouth in the name of Jesus. And I pray that You give both husband and wife peace that You will vindicate their cause. They will know that You are Jehovah Sabaoth, the Lord of Hosts. Victory belongs to You Jesus. All the glory belongs to You Jesus. You will get the glory in this situation. I decree and declare peace in the atmosphere in Jesus' name I pray, Amen."

"Amen," Tahira says in agreement.

"My daughter, you were given specific instructions. Trust God. Before this month is over the situation will be resolved. I would encourage you to pray and fast. Start by repenting. I have said what I came here to say, the rest is up to you. I love you very much sweetie." She kisses her forehead. "It is well."

As soon as the minister leaves, Tahira sobs.

Chapter

28

124 *Not So Happily Ever After*

Kian-Jion Delta, Vias

*T*avario evaded his family's calls long enough. He finally decided to fly out to visit them.

Upon opening the door, Avela hugs her son and kisses his cheeks. "My baby, I've missed you."

Tavario sinks into his mother's embrace. No matter how old he was, there was nothing like his mother's love.

"Where is my daughter?" Avela inquires, looking for Tahira.

"Fortazonio," Tavario drawls.

"I have food prepared. Are you hungry?"

"I'd never refuse your food, mom."

"Put your bags down," she replies, escorting her son to the kitchen.

"Where are dad and Tavanio?" He takes a swig of his *Passion Fruit Blitz* and begins to pick at his *Honeysuckle Short Ribs*.

"They went to play paintball. Care to explain to me why your wife isn't with you?"

Tavario reluctantly chews the meat. "I'm sure you've seen the news and the public spectacle my life has become."

Avela stares at her son. "You know that I don't pay attention to the tabloids. Any information about my family has to come from their mouths."

"I don't even know where to start."

"We've taught you children about handling your marital issues with your spouse and God's help. I try not to meddle, that's why I haven't asked. Your demeanor has changed. Tell me what's going on."

"Yo bro, you back in town?"

Tavario daps his brother. "How was paintball?"

"Dad won as usual," Tavanio laughs. He grabs a bottle of water out of the fridge. "That man's relentless. Why are you here?"

"I can't visit the old stomping grounds?"

"Oh please. Ever since you got married and became a big shot Missions Director you don't have time for us. What's up?"

"My wife and I haven't lived together for three months," Tavario blurts to his brother.

"Seriously?" Tavanio puts the bottle down.

"Does anyone in this family watch the news?"

"Is there something we should know about? You know how mom raised us; *'unless it's from the source it doesn't count.'*"

Tavario shares his ordeal with his brother.

"That's crazy man. I'm sorry. We can pray about it now if you want."

"Sure," Tavario replies. "I need all the prayers I can get."

Turning over in his bed, Tavario groans at the piercing sound of his phone ringing. "Huh... Hello?"

"I heard you're back in town."

"Who is this?"

"The mother of your son."

Tavario bolts up in irritation. "Nova, how'd you get this number?"

"I'm Nova Duesing. I have my ways. You'd be surprised how many people are willing to help a beautiful damsel in distress. Act like you know who I am," she croons.

"Is there a point to this call? What do you want?"

"Since you're here, I thought it'd be fitting that Haselt meet his grandparents, aunts, and uncles."

Tavario rubs the tension in his temples. "What is wrong with you? Stop contacting me. Go and find that boy's real father. Do you even care about his well-being, feeding him all these lies?"

127 *Not So Happily Ever After*

"How dare you! I have my son's best interest at heart. He should meet his paternal family; after all these years of not knowing them."

"Whose fault is that?"

"I'm not trying to start an argument with you, babes," Nova counters.

"Don't call me that. We're not together, I'm a married man."

"I heard there's an impending divorce on the horizon."

"Take that lie back to whoever told you."

"My sources are credible."

"Nova, it's 2AM. Can this wait until later? We need to get to the bottom of this situation once and for all."

"Now you're talking. I'll see you later then."

"That's not what I said... Nova? Nova?"

Lord please... HELP! This has got to stop.

Chapter

29

129 *Not So Happily Ever After*

5:30am

" **W**ho could be at the door so early in the morning? Avela are you expecting anyone?"

"No my love."

Evasio walks to open the door. "Nova? What brings you to our house at this hour?"

"Hi Mr. Mikos, I'm here to see Tavario. I've brought his son to meet the family."

"Who's at the door?" Avela inquires, wiping her hands on a kitchen towel. "Oh it's Nova. Why don't you come in? It's too early for you to be outside. Who is this?"

"Haselt, meet your grandparents, Evasio and Avela Mikos."

Avela smiles weakly. "Let's not start any introductions until we know for sure. I've made breakfast, are you hungry?"

"Yes," Haselt claps.

"We left home quickly this morning. I figured we'd eat breakfast with Tavario."

"I was just about to set the table for the family to eat. You can
 join us," Avela replies.

"I appreciate the hospitality. Where's Tavario?" Nova asks, looking up the stairs.

"He's asleep. He had a rough night. We'll meet you in the dining room."

"Okay Ms. Avela."

Evasio looks at his wife and whispers, "We need to pray. Tavario isn't going to want her around."

"Neither do I, but we must show them the love of Christ."

Tavario walks into the dining room wiping his hair with a towel.

"Guess who's here?" Tavanio exclaims, shaking his head.

"Good morning." Tavario greets, trying not to allow Nova to disturb his peace.

Nova grins. "Tavario, I brought Haselt to meet his family."

"Can you all excuse us?" Tavario glares at Nova. "A word, please."

Nova excuses herself from the table, smiling from ear to ear.

When they exit the dining room, Nova grabs Tavario's hands, but he immediately pulls away from her.

"What gives?"

Nova bats her eyes innocently. "I don't understand."

"First you call me at 2AM, now you're here in my family's home before the sun's even up?"

"I told you my plans."

"You don't have any rights here. You think this is some kind of game?"

"Is everything alright?" Evasio chimes, moments later.

"I don't want to be anywhere near this woman," Tavario barks.

"Remain calm, son."

"Why is she here, dad?"

Nova blinks her eyes innocuously. "Is it wrong that I want my son to spend time with his family?"

"I'm not doing this." Tavario walks upstairs in a huff.

"I've never seen him behave like this," Nova chuckles. "I just want my son to bond with everyone, is that so wrong Mr. Mikos?"

"Let's go finish breakfast. I will speak to him," Evasio announces.

"I can go talk to him."

Evasio gently pulls her back into the dining room. "**I will speak to him.**"

"*You've reached the Zagori household. No one's available at this time to answer your call. Please leave your name, number, and a brief message.*"

"*Dolcezza* please pick up. I miss you. I love you. Tahira? Tahira? I know you can hear me. Sigh! I won't stop fighting for us..."

Chapter

30

*A*n hour later, Avela walks towards the door.

"Where are you going?" Tavario inquires.

"To spend time with Nova and Haselt," she replies.

Tavario stares at his mother in shock.

"I'll be right with you, Nova," she says. "You can go wait by the car."

Nova nods. "Okay Ms. Avela. Haselt, we're going to have a family day."

"Yayyyy," Haselt squeals, swinging his mother's hand.

When they exited, Tavario turns to his mother. "What are you doing? Why are you indulging her?"

"I trust God that it will all work out. We need to be Christ-like no matter the situation. I know that you're hurting and it's challenging, but God is in charge."

"Christ-like I get, but why are you going anywhere with her? You'll plant more pseudo ideas in her head. This is the woman who is trying to destroy my marriage; the woman who has tainted my image."

Avela touches his arm. "You're a man of prayer, keep praying. God will vindicate you."

"And you think this is the way?"

"There's one thing that Nova and I have in common and because of that I understand her."

"What's that?"

"We're both mothers. And a mother would do anything for her child."

"You're empathizing with a psychopath?"

"Watch your words. Good can come from this."

"I want her out of my life for good."

Avela looks him in the eye. "My son, I know that you can't see past your nose and you want to get back to your life with your wife, but I feel the need to reach out to Nova. She needs help. She needs Jesus and if I can point her to HIM, I will. I have her trust."

"You and your compassion," Tavario shakes his head.

"You're compassionate too, but it's hitting close to home so it's harder."

"Be careful."

"I'm not afraid of Nova."

"Do I have to go?" Tavario groans, hours later.

"Come on bro. We're talking laser tag. You need to relax."

"Easy for you to say, your wife hasn't left you."

"That's why I'm in no rush to get married," Tavanio replies.

"How comforting."

"The last time we were all together was for your wedding. August and Hashir are meeting us. Let us celebrate this rare occasion that our sisters let their husbands go out," Tavanio chuckles.

When they returned from laser tag, Tavario's family gathered at the Mikos' household for lunch.

Teviva, one of his older sisters, kisses Evasio's cheek as she puts her plate out for more food. "No one can make a burger like you, dad."

Evasio smiles as he tosses more hotdogs on the grill. "Thank you, baby girl."

Tevaia nudges Tavario. "Cheer up lil bro."

"How can I cheer up?" Tavario huffs. "My marriage is in disarray, close to ending."

"That's not the Tavario I know."

"I've been praying for months and my situation is yet to change." He glances over at Nova and Haselt sitting with his mother and brother. "Nova keeps coming around. I don't want her here."

"Have you considered what you'd do if he is your son?" Tevaia poses.

"To be honest sis, I don't believe he is my son. Nova cannot be trusted. There are things I haven't told you about her."

Tevaia laughs. "I know more than you think."

"Like what?"

"That doesn't matter. Don't focus on her. Your wife and marriage is what's important. Keep your focus on Jesus and HE will work this out."

"I love how everyone's so confident when it's not happening to them," Tavario counters.

"Hey, we all have our crosses to bear, but one thing I know for sure is that God never gives us more than we can handle. Don't worry; your wife will come back to you," she squeezes his hand. "Coming Hashir," Tevaia calls out to her husband.

"I brought this for you; a peace offering." Nova hands Tavario a plate of food.

"No thank you."

"Please don't be mad at me. I've been trying for us to be a family. What do you want from me?"

"A paternity test," Tavario demands, walking away from her.

Chapter

31

*A*round 8PM, Tahira heard noise coming from the living room. "Movie night? What y'all watching?"

"Your wedding video," Tahiti chimes.

Tahira stands in front of her parents. "Why?"

"We thought it'd be great to reminisce on happier times, when you were smiling," Ramiro adds.

"Scoot over." Tahira motions to sit between her parents.

Tahiti hands her a plate filled with *Cheese Floats*.

Ramiro clicks the remote and they all journey back to the day Tahira became a Mikos.

> *"I, Tavario Eaurelius Mikos, take thee, Tahira, to be my wedded wife, to have and to hold, from this day forward, for better, for worse, for richer, for poorer, in sickness and in health, to love and to cherish, till death do us part, according to God's holy ordinance; and thereto I pledge myself to you. I promise to always treat you like the Empress that you are..."*

> *"I, Tahira Inielle Aiyoki Zagori, take thee, Tavario, to be my wedded husband, to have and to hold, from this day forward, for better, for worse, for richer, for poorer, in sickness and in health, to love and to cherish, till death do us part, according to God's holy ordinance; and thereto I pledge myself to you. And I promise mmmm hmmm mmmm to ALWAYS view you as the FINENESS that you are..."*

> *"Tahira and Tavario, by their solemn promises, freely made before God and in the presence of this*

assembly, have joined themselves to one another for love and for life.

Those whom God has joined together, let no one put asunder. By the authority vested in me by the Holy Spirit
and Country of Fortazonio, I now pronounce you husband and wife. Tavario you may now kiss your bride."

Tavanio zooms in on his sister-in-law. "How does it feel to become an official member of the Mikos clan?"

The world's biggest blush forms on Tahira's face. "I've been smiling all day. I'm happy that you're now my lil bro."

"Hey, hey, I'm not that much younger than you and Tavario."

"Will you catch the garter tonight?"

"Not a chance. I'm enjoying my singleness for as long as I can."

"There are plenty of pretty women here," Tahira hints.

"My future wife is special; I'll know her when I meet her."

Tavario strolls up and embraces his wife in a passionate kiss.

"Yo," Tavanio chuckles. "Save some for the honeymoon."

Batting away the camera, Tavario laughs. "Get outta here. I want to dance with my beautiful Empress."

"Yeah, yeah," Tavanio grins as he walks away.

Wiping her eyes, Tahira stands up.

Tahiti hands her daughter a tissue. "What's the matter?"

"Did you just see what I saw?"

Tahiti glances at the screen. "Your wedding video?"

"I see a man who loves me. And I'm here behaving like a possessed lunatic. After all I've done to him, he still pursues me. He called me last night. I don't care what that paternity test says, Tavario is MY HUSBAND and I love him. I have to fix this."

"What are you going to do?" her mother beams.

"First, I'm going to beg God for forgiveness for my ignorance and my mouth. And every negative thing I spoke into the atmosphere. It's time to get my husband back; I've left him for too long."

"HALLELUJAH," Ramiro exclaims, jumping off the couch.

Tahiti hugs her daughter. "Go do what you have to do. Your father and I will continue to pray."

Chapter

32

143 *Not So Happily Ever After*

*T*urning off all devices and shutting all the windows, Tahira gears up for a time of intense prayer. Enough was enough. No more allowing the enemy to make a mockery of her God-ordained marriage to the man she loved with her entire being.

"Dear God, I come to You in the name of Jesus repenting of my sins. Father I have sinned against You and Your word and I am sorry. Forgive me for **every** negative word that I spoke against my life and marriage. Forgive me for not taking heed to all the warnings You've sent me. I don't deserve Your forgiveness. I don't deserve You intervening on behalf of me for my marriage, but I humbly beg You to defend our marriage. I'm not strong enough to fight. I've done and said many things that rendered my marriage vows null, but Father please have mercy on me. I pray against **every** negative word that the doctors spoke over my life.

I **rebuke** PCOS right now in the name of Jesus. I renounce **every** sickness, disease, illness and ailment spoken over my life. I don't accept anything but Your word that by Your stripes I am healed. Lord You know the schemes and plots to destroy my marriage in the form of Nova Duesing. Father, I pray that if Haselt is not... Sigh... I pray that if he is not Tavario's son, that you will expose that woman's lies. Oh God, if he is Tavario's son, give me the grace and patience to deal with this change in our marriage. It wouldn't be easy, but I trust You Lord. I want to pass this test.

I pray Lord Jesus that You soften my husband's heart towards me, even after the many months that I have pushed him away. Please help him to still love me and want to work things out. Please help him to forgive me. Forgive me Jesus for how horribly I have treated the one You've blessed me with. Jesus, help me to be a better wife to him. I don't deserve Your love. I still can't fathom how

You love me Lord. I don't understand how my husband still pursues me even after all I've done. God You know how much I love Tavario. I don't want to be with anyone else. I don't want him to be with anyone else. Lord have Your way in this situation. I pray that our marriage bond will be stronger than ever as a result of all we've endured for the past few months. Help me to forgive myself for the huge part that I played in our marital downfall. I pray that You would help me to **censor** my mouth from now on. I pray that You will restore all the months of ministry that did not happen as a result of my disobedience. Have Your way in our lives Jesus. Only You can show me the way God. Guide me oh Savior. Thank You for the peace that You've placed in my heart even now. In Jesus' name I pray, Amen."

Chapter

33

*T*avario bids farewell to his family.

"I am happy that we got to spend this time with you. I'm sad that you have to leave us."

"I have to go set my house in order, mom. Prepare for Tahira's return."

"You're sure she's coming back?"

"I woke up with a peace that she will return to me," Tavario says.

"And that my son is the faith I want you to hold on to. No matter how long it takes, keep trusting God," Avela smiles.

"I love you all." Tavario hugs his parents.

"Ready to go, bro?" Tavanio dangles the car keys.

"Be careful with my son," Avela states, while she side hugs Evasio.

"I'm your son too."

"First boy," Tavario laughs. "No need to be jealous bro."

"Whatever man, let's go."

When her sons leave the house Avela breathes a sigh of relief. "I pray that Tahira returns home. Tavario is a wreck without her."

"That's how a man should love his wife," Evasio winks.

She kisses her husband. "Like how you love me?"

"Indeed my love."

"What are you gonna do when you get back to *Lux Point Milano*? You've been away from ministry and work for a long time," Tavanio asks his brother.

"Thankfully my team is understanding and has been holding down the fort while I sort things out."

"Is this what I'll have to look forward to when I'm married?"

"You can't prepare for certain issues in marriage," Tavario reveals. "You prayerfully tackle them when they come."

"But you're good right?"

"What do you mean?"

Tavanio laughs while drumming the steering wheel to the music in the background. "Bro, I've never seen you cry this much."

Punching his brother's arm, Tavario retorts, "When you meet your wife and fall in love you'll understand."

"You're whipped."

"Just keep your eyes on the road," Tavario chuckles.

Avela tossed and turned that night. Sleep eluded her.

"You're a liar. You're a liar," she calls out. "You want to ruin his life. You will be exposed..."

"Wake up. Avela wake up." Evasio gently shakes his wife as he watches the tears fall from her eyes.

"What?" she blurts, groggily.

"You were screaming and crying in your sleep."

Avela props up on her elbows.

Someone knocks on the door.

"Come in," Evasio calls.

"Mom, dad, is everything alright?" Tavanio rubs his eyes as he enters. "I heard screaming."

Evasio walks over to the door, stopping him midway. "It's okay son. Your mom had a bad dream, that's all. Go back to sleep."

"Are you sure she's okay?"

"I'm here. Don't worry about it."

Tavanio yawns. "If you all need anything—"

"Thanks my boy," he says, closing in the door. Evasio plops back on the bed. "What did you dream about?"

"I saw Nova with a strange man. I don't know who he is, but Haselt looks like him."

"Are you sure about this, Avela?"

"Yes I am. My dreams have been accurate in the past. What if she is lying, wanting to ruin our son's life and his marriage?"

"I understand that this issue has to be resolved, but it isn't our place. Tavario is a grown man and needs to handle this."

"He will always be my baby."

"I know." Evasio clasps her hands affectionately.

"I'm going to call him and tell him what I dreamed."

"Stay right there. I'll go get your phone."

Chapter

34

151 *Not So Happily Ever After*

*T*ahiti knocks on her daughter's door the following night. "Tahira, are you ready?"

"I don't see the need for me to dress up to go in the backyard."

"We want to take photos in the gazebo. I know how you get about your looks in pictures. Come on."

"Ok mom, I'll be right down."

"SURPRISE!" the women of *Fortazonio House of Worship* announces when Tahira opens the backdoor.

Tahira observes the beautiful ambience; white and gold themed with soft touches of pink and blue décor, created for a Prince and Princess.

"What's this for?" Tahira cries.

Tahiti clinks her glass. "Settle down ladies." She motions for Tahira to sit on a throne. "My daughter, we are throwing you an expectant mother's baby shower. We've been praying and agree that it is time to put our faith into action. We all love you, so we've purchased items that you'd need for a baby. Since we don't know what gender your baby will be we decided to buy neutral clothing. You have everything to decorate your nursery back home. All arrangements have been made for the items to be shipped and delivered to your home in *Lux Point Milano*."

"I-I can't believe you all would do something like this for me. A faith based baby shower?" Tahira wipes the tears from her eyes. She sighs. "These few months have been a challenge and I don't deserve any of this."

"It's our gift to you my daughter," Ankara utters. "We know that you've been praying and trying to have a baby. God knows when the time is right, but we are exercising faith, preparing for the arrival of your precious baby."

Tahira glances at her mother. "This is what you've been up to all day?"

"Yes," she giggles. "You know I'm planner extraordinaire; only the best for my baby girl."

"I'm not pregnant yet," Tahira counters.

"A woman doesn't wait until the day she gets married to purchase her wedding dress," Ankara chimes.

Tahira exhales as the reality set in. "With all this faith going around, I'll join you in believing God."

"A toast to mommy Tahira Mikos," Tahiti raises her glass. "May she give birth to beautiful babies who would grow up to be Ambassadors for Christ. May her story and testimony inspire many women for years to come."

"TO TAHARIA. MOTHER OF NATIONS," the women at the shower cheers.

"Tahira please stand. Ladies let's surround our sister as we pray for her womb to bring forth children. I'd like to ask the Women's Ministry Director, Sis. Nedeau to pray for Tahira," Minister Hizaor requests, as she and Tahiti place their hands on Tahira's stomach.

153 *Not So Happily Ever After*

"Father God, we come to You in the name of Jesus declaring that You are the Great I Am. Declaring oh Lord that there is none that compares to You. Thank You Father for who You are. Thank You Father for Your love, mercy, grace, and forgiveness. Lord we don't deserve anything, but Your word says in Jeremiah 29:11 that You know the plans You have for us... plans to prosper us and not to harm us, plans to give us hope and a future. Lord You are in control of our future. You have created each one of us for a purpose.

God, I bring Your daughter Tahira before You. Lord You know all that has transpired in her life these past few months. You know the struggle that she has endured to conceive. Lord You are her healer. Whatever the doctors have declared over her life SHALL NOT be her portion in Jesus' name. We decree and declare that You will expose EVERY lie of the enemy against the Mikos' marriage. We rebuke EVERY tongue that has risen up against them. We decree and declare a healthy body...healthy organs. We pray against barrenness in the name of Jesus. We speak **double anointing.**

A double blessing for Your daughter in Jesus' name. Guard her mind against negative thinking. Let her drink from Your living water. Meditate on Your word day and night. Let her lips speak Your word and truth ONLY. God we give You praise for turning around this situation. We thank You for Your awesome power. We decree and declare that Your name will be glorified in Tahira and Tavario's lives in the name of Jesus. I pray God that their marriage will be stronger than ever as a result of what they've gone through. Hmmmm. God I pray that You prepare Tahira for those motherless children that You will send her way. Hmmmm.

154 *Not So Happily Ever After*

Mother of Nations. Her children will call her blessed.

The Mikos' will house orphans and raise them to serve You. God You know all and I thank You for fellowshipping with us Your children. Bless each and every woman present here who may be going through her own struggle. I pray that You would intervene on her behalf. I pray that You would show up and show off in her their lives. Bless this household Lord Jesus. Even as the Zagoris would have opened their home for us to bless Your daughter. Thank You Lord for our leaders, Pastor and Minister Hizaor. May they continue to represent You in all that they do. In Jesus' name I pray, Amen."

"Amen," all the women echo when Sis. Nedeau concludes her prayer.

"Time to open presents," Tahiti squeals.

Chapter

35

"*N*o Tahira, don't go in there," Tavario rushes to stop her from opening the door.

"Why do you have a paintbrush?"

"I was trying to surprise you."

"With?"

"I guess I should show you." Tavario opens the door. Inside, the room was decorated like an airport. There were inscriptions of scripture verses written in gold lettering.

"What is this?" Tahira asks.

"It's a nursery," Tavario replies.

"I'm not pregnant, *Miore*."

"This is preparation for when the time comes. I don't want our baby to come as a surprise, so I'm preparing."

Walking over to the rocking chair, Tahira sits and cries rubbing her belly. "We'll continue to pray and trust God for our baby."

"You're not mad?" he inquires.

"There's no reason to be mad. This is a beautifully thoughtful gesture." She stands up and hugs his waist. "I love you, *Miore*. You're the best husband in the world."

"I can't wait to see you hold a mini me in your arms."

"Who said the baby will be a boy?"

"Of course our first child will be a boy."

"That's what you want. God may have other plans."

"God knows my heart's desire," he smiles.

"I want a girl."

"Either way, I'll be happy. You're going to make a lovely mother," Tavario says, kissing her forehead.

Oh no. It was only a dream. Father God, please guide me. All these prayers and dreams. Only You know what they mean. I trust You. Speak to Tavario's heart even now. Sigh! I miss Miore...

Chapter

36

"*M*r. Mikos there's a package on your desk. Welcome back to work," Tavario's secretary greets, the next afternoon.

"I'm glad to be back, Cypress."

"Will Mrs. Mikos be joining us for lunch?"

"She hasn't returned yet," Tavario tells the woman.

"We're all praying for you, sir."

"Thanks," he smiles weakly.

Tavario pours himself a cup of *Cobalt Tea* and proceeds to sit down. Hiring the PI was a last resort for him. Nova refused all his efforts to do the DNA test, so he hired a lawyer and PI to get the information that he needed. One way or the other this situation dragged on for too long and he couldn't sit by and watch his marriage go up in flames. After prayer, he was led to contact the two men who aided him in his investigation; two brothers from their church, so he trusted them.

After reading the reports of their findings, he turns to the page containing the DNA information.

Vias Biolabs

Case Ref: TA2345678
Date: 07.20.2024

DNA PROFILING TEST RESULTS

Alleged Father: Tavario Mikos

Name of Mother: Not Tested

Name of Child: Haselt Duesing

ALLEGED FATHER	PROBABILITY OF PATERNITY
Tavario Mikos	0%

Report

An assessment of the DNA profiles of Tavario Mikos and Haselt Duesing does not support the premise that Tavario Mikos is the biological father of Haselt Duesing. Based on the testing results obtained from the analysis of the DNA loci listed in the data, the probability of paternity is 0%.

All testing has been performed based on information provided by the client.

Conclusion

The probability of paternity is 0%; this excludes Tavario Mikos as the biological father of Haselt Duesing.

161 *Not So Happily Ever After*

Chapter

37

$\mathcal{B}$REAKING NEWS: "Shocking DNA results. Earlier this month, 28 year old Vias supermodel, Nova Duesing accused former actor Tavario Mikos of being a deadbeat father. We've recently discovered that this was a lie. Tavario is **NOT** the father of Nova's 7 year old son, Haselt Duesing. Sources say that the biological father of Nova's son is none other than 50 year old photographer, Ndali Arganbright with whom Nova had an affair with while dating Mr. Mikos. Mr. Arganbright who has been married for the past 25 years has refused to comment. His wife's Rep has asked that the public be considerate of this delicate situation concerning her husband's infidelity; which she had prior knowledge of. No comment has been made from Nova or her Rep. We're all rooting for the Mikos'. Tavario was a well-loved actor and we are happy that the truth has been brought to light. And now, back to your regularly scheduled program..."

Tahiti grabs her daughter in excitement. Tahira then drops to the floor and cries.

"HE did it. God vindicated us. Now the world knows the truth. This woman's lies have been exposed. God I thank You. God I thank You." Tahira exclaims while walking around the living room.

Ramiro begins to play a song of praise on the piano.

"Praise God from whom all blessings flow." Tahiti joins her husband in praise. "Honey, you should call your husband now. Celebrate this victory together."

"I'll do one better. I'm going to book a flight for tomorrow night."

"After all you've been through, I am glad that you got this good news," Tahiti replies.

God I thank You for all that You've done. Thank You for exposing the lies and deception of the enemy. Even in the midst of my joy, I pray God that You will help me to forgive Nova for what she has done. I pray that Haselt would not be emotionally distraught by the actions of his parents. I haven't been home in months and I don't know what I am going back to. Please soften Tavario's heart towards me and help us to reconcile our marriage...

Chapter

38

165 *Not So Happily Ever After*

"*G*irl, I saw the news. How do you feel? Not only has Nova been exposed on national television, but Tavario's name has been cleared," Kaiora screams excitedly over the phone.

"It feels wonderful. I've been away from home for a long time. So much has changed and I am glad that it's ending on a happy note. For some strange reason I feel sorry for Nova."

"That's the compassion that can only come from the Lord. In and of ourselves we wouldn't feel anything but hate towards our enemies. Her son is who will be mostly affected by this. I pray it wouldn't have any long-term repercussions. Tahira? Tahira? Are you there?"

"Sorry Kaiora, I just got this sharp pain in my belly."

"How long have you been feeling this way?"

"The pain came on suddenly. It's been weeks since I've felt it."

"Are you sure that you're not pregnant?"

"All the tests that I've done to this point has returned negative."

"But this isn't normal. Besides what's been said, I think that you're pregnant."

"I don't have time to go to the doctor. My flight's tonight."

"TAHIRA! Go to the doctor. I don't want anything to happen to you en route to the airport or while you're on the plane. I know you want to get back to your husband, but your health is important—"

"Let's not think negative," Tahira stops Kaiora mid thoughts. "I've gotten in enough trouble for my mouth."

"Understandable, but you must exercise wisdom. If you won't listen, I'll call your mother to take you."

"Okay, okay, Kaiora. I'll go."

"Thank you. I just finished speaking with Amerigio. He has a meeting with the Crown Prince."

"I can't believe he's friends with royalty."

"Apparently the prince's wife is originally from Starr Islands."

"Maybe Nayoro will become a princess."

"Wouldn't that be something?" Kaiora chuckles. "Thank God she's already royalty."

"Aren't we all—"

"I gotta go. Let me know what happens at the doctor. I love you. Muahz!"

"I love you," Tahira replies.

Chapter

39

*T*ahira hated traveling in the rain. She prayed that the flight wouldn't be delayed. After all this time apart, she was eager to return to her husband.

Saying goodbye to her parents was not easy, but she was excited to see Tavario again. She opted to surprise him. Hopefully, he was home and not at work or elsewhere.

Breathe Tahira breathe. Tavario loves you. He'll be glad to see you. Everything will be fine. Go to sleep. The worst is over. Only exciting news from now on...

Although he didn't like the idea of his private life being public knowledge, Tavario was thankful that he got the answers he needed. The first thing that he did was call his wife, but no one answered the phone at the Zagoris. He decided not to panic and trusted God to work things out. That news was just step one. Now he needed to reconcile with Tahira.

When the news broke, his phone rang off with calls from his family and friends; all celebrating their answered prayers. His mother's dream had indeed come true. Thanks flowed out of his lips as he praised God. He also decided to pray for the atmosphere where he resided; praying against all the negativity that transpired within the four walls.

Peace reigned in his heart as he continued to trust God for his wife to return home. Oh how he missed her. The joy she brought to his heart couldn't be compared to anything else. Growing up, he never expected to love a woman as much as he loved Tahira.

Tavario turns down the volume on the TV.

I thought I heard the bell ring. Must be my—

He gets up from the couch when he realizes that he was not hallucinating.

"Who could be at the door this hour? I don't want any more trouble," he says aloud.

Just then a bolt of thunder was heard. He was tired to say the least, but the doorbell kept ringing. Not bothering to view the video feed of the outside, he opens the door to a pleasant surprise. His wife stood on the welcome mat dripping wet, with bags in tote.

"*Dolcezzaaaaaaaa.*" He picks up his wife and spins around on the porch, then begins to kiss her fervently.

Tahira shudders. "C-can we go inside?" she says, when he puts her down.

No one could've been happier than Tavario was at that moment. The love of his life, officially back home where she belonged. He took her bags and placed them inside.

Time stood still as they stared into each other's eyes, crying. No one spoke. Words evaded the couple.

Chapter

40

*L*ater that night, Tahira and Tavario sit down on their living room couch, to discuss the past few months in their relationship. He gives her a slice of *Macadamia Cloud Torte*.

When Tahira finishes eating the torte, she wipes her mouth with a napkin.

"What did the doctor say?" Tavario repeats, remembering their initial conversation in April.

"You're not going to believe it," Tahira pauses.

"Let's not go down this road again."

"I'm going to tell you. You're just not going to believe it."

"After all we've been through *Dolcezza*; I hope its good news."

"More than good news."

"Well don't keep your husband in suspense."

"I..."

"Yes?" Tavario prods.

"I don't have PCOS," she reveals.

"Praise the Lord. That is **excellent** news. God is good to us."

"It was a misdiagnosis for something else."

"Uh oh, that doesn't sound good."

"Actually Mr. Mikos, it's **doubly good**."

Tavario stares at Tahira, the suspense eating him up. "Tell me, tell me."

"I'm... **pregnant**," she tearfully reveals.

Tavario jumps up from the couch and shouts praises to God in excitement. Then he looks at his wife. "You're having my baby?"

"**Two** babies," she holds up her fingers.

"What are you saying?" he asks.

"We're having twins."

"Wait, wait. How is this possible? You said all your tests came back negative."

"According to the doctor I visited before I boarded the plane, he'd never seen anything like my pregnancy before. Apparently, the way our children were positioned, showed up like cysts on the ultrasound, hence the earlier misdiagnosis from previous doctors. It sounds weird, I know, but... When one of the babies moved, he did another ultrasound to make sure he was seeing correct. At first there was no heartbeat, and then faint sounds and BAAM two very loud fetal heartbeats were heard. The doctor was baffled. He said our children are quite special to say the least."

Tavario begins to sing about God being a miracle worker. "I'm going to be the father of twins. Whoa. I need to sit down. Do you know their gender?"

"A mini **you** and a mini **me**."

"A boy and a girl? Praise God from whom all blessings flow."

Tahira begins to cry as she observes her husband's happiness at the news. Knowing that she was able to give him his heart's desire brought an overwhelming joy to her.

God, thank You for answering our prayers. You have not only blessed us with one, but two children. That's what the Prophetess meant by **two**.

Taking his wife's hands, Tavario begins to spin her around and they dance.

"I need to sit down," Tahira exhales.

"Sure. Sure. Anything for my wife." He kneels in front of her and places his hand on her stomach. "Hey there little ones, this is your father speaking. I love you both very much. Your mommy's a feisty one. I'm begging you both to come out like your father; cool, calm and collected. No more acrobatic stunts in the womb. I look forward to the day I get to hold you both in my arms. I promise to be the best father I can be." Tavario then kisses his wife's stomach, crying.

"It's okay *Miore*. I know this has been a tough year, but God came through for us. HE truly blesses us with more than we deserve. I couldn't have asked for a better husband. You've proven time after time that you love me like Christ loves the Church and for that I'm eternally grateful."

Tavario stares deeply into his wife's eyes. "Empress, there is no other woman for me. I'm going to spend the rest of my life loving and protecting you. Thank you for the gift of fatherhood. I wouldn't want to parent with anyone else." He kisses her passionately. "Let's go upstairs."

"Why not," she giggles. "I'm already pregnant."

"Glad that we're thinking the same thing," he winks.

They both laugh.

OTHER
BOOKS

Written By

THEASTARR
VALERIE

ROMANCE

Worth The Wait Series

How did Tahira and Tavario's love begin? It all started in **The Road That Led To Love**. Be sure to get your copy on Amazon today. Here's a sample of their
 journey.

Book 1: *The Road That Led To Love*

I never met him, but I'm completely in love with him. When I was 8 years old I saw him for the first time on TV. I watched every show and movie he acted in and swooned. He is THE definition   of FINATION. I had to make up a word to describe him. Yes, I know wishful thinking. As if I would EVER meet him. As if he would EVER like me...

"Earth to Tahira," Kaiora sings.

"We are supposed to be studying," Tahira replies.

Kaiora Marzocco had been Tahira's firecracker best friend for the past two years. Her mouth was known to get her in trouble at times; she held nothing back.

"I know that, but you zoned out. Daydreaming about that boy again?" she jeers.

"Who?" Tahira asks.

"The one you've liked since you were 8 years old."

"No. I was pondering on our exam tomorrow."

"Good. You need to learn now that it will never happen. Our life isn't a movie. Boys like that don't court or marry regular girls like us," Kaiora scolded, while popping a gum in her mouth.

Tahira stands up and declares, "I am not a regular girl. I am the daughter of a King."

"So am I, but the Bible speaks about idolatry."

"I haven't idolized anyone."

"Either way, let's stick with reality," Kaiora states nonchalantly.

"Besides, he isn't a believer."

Tahira frowns. "He does believe in Jesus."

"Believing in Jesus and serving HIM are two different things."

"Can we stop with the sermons? I know God's word," Tahira conveys, becoming agitated.

Pointing to the textbooks Kaiora ends the conversation. "Back to our studies."

Tahira begins to twiddle her fingers, zoning Kaiora out as she thinks.

Why is it so impossible for me to marry Tavario Mikos? He could become a Christian, like really serving Jesus. SIGH!! Who am I kidding? As Kaiora said, this isn't the movies...

End of Sample.

Upcoming Book in this Series

M.I.A.

Love In Lucca Series

Book 1: *Becoming a Royal Princess*

"There is no fear in love; but perfect love casteth out fear..." 1 John 4:18

Vaia throws herself on the bed; a million questions dancing around her head. Who was this man? Could she trust him?

She looked in the mirror, deciding on whether to change. Her suitcase was filled with unused garments.

I don't have time for one night flings. What do I know about this man? Am I really going on a fake date with him? This is unlike me.

Five minutes later, against her better judgment, Vaia makes her way to the 12th floor. What was the worst that could happen on a ship with numerous cameras and workers? If she felt uncomfortable, she had two choices: run or scream.

———

End of Sample.

MYSTERY

Nhyira Files Mystery Series

Book 1: Murder In Zaire Valley

Flipping through the radio stations, Nhyira Enosis puts her **Epitome X Series 1** into sports mode, excited at the chance to test drive her new car. She was minutes away from her potential dream house: a 40-year-old mansion in *Njapa, Zaire Valley,* Celgagoas.

A native of *Grape Fjord*, Mt. Thafivin, she was known as **The** Spelling Bee Champ. Nhyira had a natural ability to unscramble any word from the dictionary.

And no one could deny her fascination for unsolved mysteries. When she read the ad for the abandoned house up for auction, she knew that it had to be hers.

With her inheritance in her purse she mashed the gas pedal. If she missed the auction, someone else would bid on the house. That was a setback she couldn't afford.

Mr. Sellers had the perfect house for Nhyira. As the top Real Estate Agent in *Zaire Valley*, he knew how to match the perfect house with its perfect owner. This particular house however, remained unsold for decades. No one in the country was interested in procuring a house formerly owned by a man whose wife murdered him in cold blood.

The mystery of the old **Veisiejai House** remained since 1958. It was a part of *Njapa's* history that none of its residents dared to speak about. Only a handful
of citizens knew what *really* happened on that fateful night...

End of Sample.

Book 2: *A Fatal Bite*

An hour later, a boy comes up to Nhyira, frantic. "Miss, miss, why do you have that sign in front your diner?"

Nhyira glances at the young man nonchalantly. "Did you want something? No freebies today."

"That means you didn't see. Come look outside," the boy pulls Nhyira. "There. Look." He points to the graffiti on the storefront.

AVOID THIS DINER.
DEATH IS SERVED HERE.

Nhyira holds her head in exasperation; knowing that the man with his rebel crew spray painted this horrendous sign in front of the diner.

No wonder no one's been coming in.

End of Sample.

Follow **Empress Royále Publishing** on Facebook and Instagram for information about upcoming books from Theastarr Valerie.